Tales of the Early World

ff

TED HUGHES

Tales of the
Early World

Illustrated by Andrew Davidson

faber and faber

LONDON · BOSTON

First published in 1988
by Faber and Faber Limited
3 Queen Square, London WC1N 3AU

Photoset by Parker Typesetting Service Leicester
Printed in Great Britain by
Mackays of Chatham Ltd, Kent

'The Guardian' was first published in *Guardian Angels*,
edited by Stephanie Nettell, Viking Kestrel, 1987

British Library Cataloguing in Publication Data

Hughes, Ted
Tales of the early world.
I. Title   II. Davidson, Andrew
823'.914 [J]   PZ7
ISBN 0-571-15126-4

For Carol

Contents

How Sparrow Saved the Birds   1

The Guardian   16

The Trunk   30

The Making of Parrot   37

The Invaders   51

The Snag   63

The Playmate   72

The Shawl of the Beauty of
     the World   85

Leftovers   95

The Dancers   111

How Sparrow Saved the Birds

Of all the birds, Sparrow was one of the first to be invented. Plain little Sparrow. He lived with his wife in a hole in a tree, and sometimes sat in his doorway singing his plain little song – which isn't really a song at all.

Sparrow and his wife had no children. 'It's God's fault,' cried his wife. 'Go to God and tell him so. Tell him to do something about it.' And she burst into tears. 'Surely he'll help us.'

Instead, Sparrow went to the Toad. The Toad was already making a name for herself as a witch. From her, he bought a powerful spell.

'When this spell fails to bring twins,' said the Toad, 'it brings triplets.'

Then she blinked her great, brilliant, golden eyes and added: 'Octuplets have been known.'

But it didn't work.

Sparrow's wife wept a lot, in her dark hole in the tree. 'Go to God,' she sobbed. 'Simply go to God. That's all there is to it. Why not? Go and ask him for help.'

Sparrow glared at his wife, frowning under his black thinking-cap. He was actually quite a fierce-looking little bird. His wife was right. Why not go to the top?

So he filled his knapsack with seeds, food for a very long journey, and he set off.

God was still making birds. Since making Sparrow, he'd enlarged his designs a good deal, and brought in some new ideas. He'd built a new workshop too, on stilts, on top of a hill, so the new birds would get a good take-off.

And at last Sparrow was climbing the rickety ladder to the workshop. As he got to the top rung, and peered in through the open door, a great flurry of white cloud came out. He glimpsed a small, round, black eye, then he was knocked backwards. He fell five rungs and clung there, while the giant form of a white Swan laboured out into the air, with its weird, slow wingbeats – each wingbeat giving the yelp of a hound. Sparrow stared at the whiteness, the slowness, the long neck. 'And probably,' he thought, 'it has a beautiful song too!'

He climbed back to the top, but again as he lifted his head to peer into the workshop another Swan came hurtling out. This time he ducked, then watched as the two Swans together side by side circled the tower, on their yelping wings. He watched, until they turned and flew out over the deep green valleys towards the blue curve of the world's edge. What flyers! And where were they going? What adventure!

He suddenly remembered where he was. Bracing himself, he stepped into the workshop where God was bent over his workbench.

'Hello, God,' called Sparrow, and stood.

God went on working. He was concentrating deeply on a very tricky job. Under his hands lay the first

Curlew, and he was trying to adjust its voice-box so the song would go up at the end.

Sparrow scraped his clawy foot on the floor and coughed. Then again he shouted: 'Hello, God, it's me, your old Sparrow!'

God uttered a cry, and jerked his hands up as if his fingers had been stung. Then he grabbed his hair in his fists.

'No!' he roared. 'Oh no!'

Sparrow coughed, and again shouted: 'God!'

God turned sharply and glared at him.

'You!' he suddenly bellowed. 'You made me do it. I thought I was hearing voices but it was you! I've snapped it. Now it will never be right! Oh no!'

And he turned back to peer into the throat of the Curlew.

'God,' shouted Sparrow again, 'I've come – '

'What do you want?' God was glaring at him angrily.

Sparrow took a deep breath. 'Well, God, we're only Sparrows, I know, but my wife and I would like a nestling or two or even three if it's possible because – '

'Go away!' shouted God. 'Not today. Some other time. Sparrows! I can't think about Sparrows. I'm on Curlews! And Sanderlings are coming up any minute. Go away.'

And he bent low over the Curlew with the damaged voice-box.

Sparrow didn't move. He didn't know what to do. If he went home, what would his wife feel? At the same time, he didn't dare to ask God again.

'I'll stand here,' he thought, 'until he's finished. However long that may be.'

But at that very moment, a rushing wall of twigs hit

3

him. God's mother was tidying and her broom swept Sparrow straight out through the doorway.

He flew down and landed on a rock, blinking the dust out of his eyes. What now?

Well, maybe he would wait here. One thing was sure: he wasn't going to give up, till God had listened to him in a patient, thoughtful way.

A Curlew swooped out of the workshop and then climbed away. Its wobbling, thin, whistling cry trailed away downward at the end, broken.

Sparrow sat on, through that day. He watched Sanderlings fling out of God's workshop, in twos, followed by Golden Plover, followed by Snipe. Then a Gannet, with funny, stiff-looking wings, like boards, and horrible pale little eyes at the corners of its mouth. The eye pupils were tiny as pinpricks.

The world was filling up with birds. Already, the motes tossing in clouds from hill to hill, over the valleys, were birds. The deep throbbing and thrilling voice of the forests was actually birds. The lakes were sprinkled and dimpled with birds. The edge of the sea, where the breakers tore into blowing tatters, was a lifting and falling commotion of birds. And high above, suspended from the blue, the slow, dark, circling crosses were birds.

And still God went on creating more. And more. And more.

He had a passion for birds!

Then towards the evening, as the sun lowered its red ball towards the cold Western sea, God came out on to his veranda, at the top of his ladder, and held up his hands, cupped together. Sparrow had been dozing, but now he woke with a jerk, and watched closely. What was God up to?

4

God threw up his hands gently and opened them. A peculiar black shape whizzed out of them. Sparrow blinked. He thought God had thrown a boomerang at him. It seemed to be black spinning blades going at terrific speed, and it dived down straight at Sparrow, then:

Fffffwwwt!

It whacked past his head and shot up into the sky – just like a boomerang. But it wasn't a boomerang. It was a real bird.

God stood laughing softly with joy, as the bird spun away into the world. Sparrow could see he was almost weeping, his eyes were moist, as if he could hardly believe what he saw.

'I did it!' cried God. And he looked down at Sparrow and pointed at the vanishing marvel. 'I did it! I made a Swift!'

'Now,' thought Sparrow, 'now is my moment. He's in a joyful mood. He's just brought off a winner. He'll be feeling easy-going and generous. I'll land on his shoulder and nibble his ear, and make my request.'

And he flew up off the rock.

But at that instant, the sun touched the Western sea. A strange, rumbling quake spread over the waters, and came across the lands, and above it a darkness, full of lightnings. Sparrow checked his flight and hovered in mid-air, amazed to see the forests swirling like water. Then he saw God clutch his doorpost, while his tower swayed like a palm tree.

That was the last thing Sparrow saw, before the blackness snatched him up.

Then he was whirling in a blackness. All round him he could hear birds, crying and screeching, the fright-cries of the birds! He was no longer trying to fly. He folded his wings tightly, and tucked up his feet, and squeezed his head down between his shoulders, and peered out over his eyelids. Now and again a feathery body struck him. He knew he was whirling in a cloud of birds, a black bagful of birds. Were they all in a sack? Were they all being carried off in a great bag?

Something God had never heard about, a Black Hole in space, had lowered its whirling snout to the earth, like an Elephant's trunk. First it had blown all the birds off their perches, and out of their bushes, then it had sucked them up in one whoosh – a spinning whoosh. Like water going out of a plug-hole downwards, all the birds of the world were whirling into the Black Hole upwards. They were being hoovered up.

And in a few minutes they were gone. The world was emptied of birds.

God wandered over the hills, calling to the birds. Every single one had gone. Or so it seemed to God. He just couldn't believe it. Actually, one bird was left. The Burrow Owl. Two big yellow eyes stared upwards from the bottom of its black burrow. But it wouldn't come out. No, not even to comfort God. It stayed where it was, waiting for the next terrible blast of black wind.

God sat down on a ridge, his elbows on his knees, clutching the roots of his hair in his hands, and watching the tears splash into the dust between his feet as he sobbed. He really felt his heart was broken this time.

How could he begin again? How could he ever create a Hummingbird again? Or a Sparrow-hawk? Or a Skylark? Or a Wren? Or a Kingfisher? Or a Snow Bunting?

As he recited their names, new sobs shook him. The

6

animals gazed at him in fear and went past softly. The worms drew back into their holes. The flies crept under leaves.

And in the lakes, and in the rivers, and in the sea, the fish hung motionless, listening round-eyed, hearing through all the shaking curtains of water the heartbroken sobbing of God.

'Where are they?' he suddenly roared. 'Who has stolen my birds?'

But God knew nothing about the Black Hole. So he never guessed where they might have gone. It was a total mystery. He wandered about, stunned. He stopped making things. He lay full length beside the sea, his forearm over his eyes, and he looked as if he'd died of grief, except that his fists were tightly clenched, and tears crept back into his ears, while all over the world the eggs in the nests went cold.

Meanwhile, the birds huddled together in the darkness. Now it had stolen them, the Black Hole seemed quite satisfied. They seemed to be in some sort of pit. The various Owls glared, trying to give a little light with their eyes. But it wasn't the sort of light any other bird could see by.

'We are in a deep, deep pit,' said the Snowy Owl. 'Don't you see?'

'It looks pretty hopeless,' said the Barn Owl.

They knew they were a vast distance from the world. But they had no idea where.

The Homing Pigeons were baffled. They turned their heads this way and that.

'Our compasses don't work,' they whimpered. 'We must be somewhere beyond the stars.'

Hearing this, many of the birds began to cry again. Then, from far above, came a laugh. A long, rippling, eerie laugh! The birds felt their feathers stick up on end and they all went dead silent.

'Who's that?' whispered a Coot.

'Now you're mine, pretty birds. My mother wanted a pretty bird. So now you all belong to my mother.'

And from high up there, somewhere in the dark, the peculiar laugh came again. The birds would have liked to look at each other. Instead, even though they were huddled together so tightly, they just stared horrified into the utter black, each on his own, each by herself.

'Sing for my mother,' said the voice then. 'Come on, let's have a cheery morning chorus.'

The birds listened in horror. Suddenly there came a bang, and all the birds crashed together in a heap, their ears ringing. The voice seemed to have slapped the pit with its hand, or maybe kicked it.

'Sing, you brats,' it screeched. And again there came a bang, and again they all turned somersaults and landed on top of each other.

'Are you going to sing?' came the screech.

Then the Crow, very quick, shouted in his worst voice:

'You've broken our voices, you big idiot. Just listen. You've broken our glottals.'

Hearing the Crow, the Black Hole thought it was true, it had broken their voices. It didn't know anything about birds.

It howled a great curse, up in the black, and fell silent. What next? What was it thinking now? All the birds waited for it to play its next dreadful trick.

And in the silence, very quietly at first, the birds began to cry again.

It was in this crying that Sparrow heard his wife. He pushed through the crush, and found her. They put their wings around each other, and sat there in the dark.

'If only God knew!' whispered his wife. 'Surely he'd help us!' But God did not know. God lay in the world, beside the booming surf, and his mind, too, was simply one big blackness.

Quite soon, the birds began to feel hungry. The Sparrow undid his knapsack, and shared his seeds. He worked his way among the tightly packed birds, and asked each one:

'Can you eat seeds?'

And in the pitch dark, the birds would answer. Sparrow gave one seed to each seed-eater. He couldn't help the insect-eaters, and the grub-eaters, such as the Wrens and the Woodpeckers. Once, coming up against a very horny, unbirdlike body, he asked: 'Do you eat seeds?' And a voice from far above his head replied, in a deep, drum-like rumble:

'I am the Monkey-eating Eagle.'

Sparrow realized he was leaning on the Eagle's ankle, and he got clear fast.

He knew this couldn't go on very long. Pretty soon, the Eagles and Owls and Hawks and Gulls would begin to eat the others. If they were all to get back to earth, it would have to be quick. Otherwise – he couldn't bear to think about it. It would be awful. It might be happening already. The sly Owls, with their night sight, were probably at it already – snatching up the nearest small bird with such a savage, sudden grip there wasn't even a gasp.

Sparrow gave out every seed except for two. One for his wife, and one for himself.

'That's it,' he whispered to her, then. 'No more seeds.'

'Are you sure?' she asked. She always wanted to make sure. So she opened his knapsack, and stuck her head inside. She pulled her head out quickly and listened.

'Do you hear the sea?' she asked.

'What?' said her husband. 'What do you mean, hear the sea?'

'Inside your bag,' she said. 'I heard the sea.'

Sparrow stuck his head inside the knapsack. And there it was. The strong, crumpling boom of heavy surf, falling on a shingly beach.

He listened, amazed. Then he realized it was coming from one corner of the knapsack. He poked down there, with his beak, and found a seed. One seed. And the sound of the sea was coming out of the seed.

He brought it out, nipped in his bill. The sound of the surf filled his head.

A sudden wild clamour went up from the Gulls somewhere in the dark. 'It's the sea!' they cried. 'The sea! Listen! It's the sea!'

All the birds shouted excitedly. And the voice of the Loon cried above them all:

'The earth is coming, the earth is looking for us! That's its panting breath, as it climbs through space!'

Sparrow turned his head this way and that. Although the sea-sound came out of the seed, he felt it was coming from one direction only. He turned towards the sound. And as he did so, a strange thing happened. He saw the sea! Tiny and far off, as if he were looking through the wrong end of a telescope.

With the seed in his bill, and the sound of the surf in

11

his ears, he saw the long shore, and the great slow combers crumbling to whiteness.

He took the seed out of his bill, and was going to tell his wife to look at the sea, but the moment he took the seed from his bill everything went dark. And though he could still hear the surf, the sea had vanished.

He put the seed back in his bill, and after twisting his head this way and that, he found the sea again. It was just as if his brain was a telescope – but only if he held the seed in his bill.

'I see the sea!' he shouted. 'I see the earth and the sea!'

As he shouted the seed fell from his beak. But he found it again, between his wife's toes, because of the noise of the surf coming out of it. He put it back in his beak, to make sure it wasn't broken. And this time he saw more. He saw the sea, the surf, and the long beach. And lying along the beach – God!

He took the seed in his claw.

'I see God!' he yelled.

All the birds went silent, listening to the sea, and hearing Sparrow's words, and trying to see something in the perfect blackness.

'Come on,' cried Sparrow. 'Follow me! Follow me! Follow the sea-sound!'

And he gripped the seed in his bill, and flew up, flying towards that vision of the sea and of God lying beside it.

It was easy to keep his direction. It was exactly like following a compass. As long as he held the seed, he simply flew towards the bright little picture of God lying beside the surf.

And with a dull roar, like another sea, all the birds flew up into the dark, and followed him. They

12

couldn't see the picture. And in that blank dark they couldn't see Sparrow. But they could hear the sea, booming out of the seed in Sparrow's bill.

So all the birds of the world set off, a rustling, immense cloud, flying through the great darkness of space, following the sound of the surf.

Far above, a voice howled: 'Come back!'

But the birds flew on, blindly. Only Sparrow could see anything. And what he saw seemed to be both very far off, and inside his head, as he held the seed. The rest flew into the pitch dark, as if their eyes were closed.

'Come back!' screeched the thin, terrible voice again, growing closer.

The Black Hole was coming after them, with its sucker.

Then it swirled in among them. It was like the nozzle of a vacuum cleaner whirling about in a dense cloud of flies. The birds felt themselves caught in the whirlwind and snatched away.

Soon, Sparrow was flying alone. He didn't know it. He thought they were all following him. He didn't dare take the seed from his bill, because he thought he might drop it into empty space. And the sound of the surf in his head made it impossible to hear the little cries of the birds as they were sucked away once again into the Black Hole.

For some reason the Black Hole couldn't get a grip on Sparrow. It tore off some of his tail feathers, but as long as he held the seed, and kept his eyes on his bright picture, it couldn't suck him in. Finally, it coiled up and whipped away with a howl, and Sparrow flew on into a faint growing light like dawn.

Now he saw he was alone. But there was nothing he could do about it. Now his only hope was to tell God. He kept going. And the light brightened.

And at last, worn out, with frayed feathers, he fell on to God's chest, swallowed the seed, and lay panting.

Imagine God's joy, when he looked down at what had dropped on his chest, and found Sparrow.

'Look!' he shouted to his mother. 'Look! Sparrow! Where have you been?'

She gave Sparrow a drink and God listened to his tale. As he listened, his frown darkened. And when Sparrow had finished, God stood up.

'An oversight,' he said grimly. 'That Black Hole has made its nest in the stars. Once it was only a little dust-devil, playing in the ashes of volcanoes. Now it's eating the stars and growing. Yes, that's what must be happening. Something I never expected! Well, we'll soon fix it, now we know what it is.'

And with those words God leaped upwards. 'Be careful!' shouted his mother. But the heavens were already rumbling. A few stars fell, in broad daylight.

God tied the Black Hole and its mother into a tight knot, and fed them to the constellation of Capricorn. Then he brought the birds home. And they spread out over the world, a thousand times more joyful than before.

God nodded and smiled. 'A very good thing!' he said. 'Some of them used to moan and grumble a lot. But after a spell in the Black Hole, now they know better.'

Then he saw Sparrow, sitting on the veranda rail of his workshop, with his wife beside him.

'As for you,' said God, 'for you there is a reward. To tell you the truth, Sparrow, I wasn't too sure about you. I thought you had it in you to be a real pest. But you've proved your quality. And this is your reward: your children shall inherit the whole earth.'

Then Sparrow put back his head and let out a song of joy, a psalm to God. And his wife, too, she lifted her beak and sang out beside him.

It sounded the same as ever. A few raspy chirrups, like a Stone-Age man trying to strike a spark between two flints, and not having much success.

But God was pleased.

Then Sparrow and his wife flew off, back to their hole in the tree, in the middle of the forest from which the singing of all the birds rose like the sound of surf.

The Guardian

Man was easy to create. God simply shaped the clay, breathed life into it, and up jumped Man, ready to go.

God smiled. 'Now,' he said, 'I'll make your better half. Then you'll be complete.'

So then God shaped Woman. He took great care, and she turned out perfect. God was pleased. But when he tried to breathe life into her – nothing happened. He tried again, breathing the life in very gently. She just lay there, lifeless clay. He shook her slightly, and frowned.

Man was watching anxiously. 'What's wrong?' he cried. God didn't answer. He only rolled Woman up into a ball between his palms, and started all over again.

This time he took even more care. And pretty soon, there she lay, more perfect than ever. So once again, God kneeled forward, and breathed life into her, more warmly and gently even than before.

Still nothing happened.

There she lay, warm from God's hands, perfectly shaped. Much more perfect than Man. But lifeless.

Man couldn't hold back any longer. 'Let me have a go!' he cried, and almost pushed God aside. He grabbed Woman by the shoulders and began to shake her. 'Wakey wakey!' he called. 'Come on! Time to go!'

Her limp body shook like a rag doll, but her eyes stayed shut.

All at once he seemed to grow angry. His hair began to fly, he ground his teeth, his eyes blazed, and God was suddenly afraid what might happen as Woman's arms flapped and flopped, and her head joggled and rolled. He caught Man's arm and jerked him away. 'Steady on!' God shouted. 'She's fragile!'

But Man began to pound the earth with his fists. 'I can't bear it!' he cried. 'Do something. She's my other half. You can't just leave her lying there on the cold ground.'

God stared at him hard. Easy enough to say 'Do something', but if life wouldn't go into this marvellous new creation of his, then it wouldn't go, and that was that. He didn't know what else he could do.

At that moment, a small bird flew down and landed on Woman's left big toe. 'Let me have a try,' said the bird. 'I have magic.'

It was the Nightingale. Nightingale had a most peculiar voice. God looked at this slim, brown, tiny creature and remembered all the trouble he'd had with the voice-box. Nightingale's voice-box was incredibly complicated. God had been struggling to get this voice-box right. And then, one night, it had come to him in a dream. The perfect voice-box! And it solved one of his toughest problems: how to get the voice of the seven seas into an organ the size of a common House-Fly. And there it was in his dream. He'd woken up with a jolt, and snatched it out of the air before it could vanish. He got it – but grabbing it like that, half asleep, he'd broken it.

And what a job that had been, trying to start it up again inside the bird's tiny throat. Still, it just about worked, finally. But the voice, wonderful as it

17

sounded, was obviously only the bits and pieces of something much more tremendous.

'Try if you like,' sighed God, and he watched gloomily as Nightingale perched on Woman's nose and began to sing.

Man had never heard the Nightingale sing. And now it really let itself go, he couldn't believe his ears. As it sang, his eyes grew very large and round. Suddenly they closed, his head dropped forward on his chest, and he was in a trance.

And a row of eight Monkeys, sitting on the branch of a tree above him, fell to the ground, bounced once, and lay still, eyes closed, in a trance.

What singing!

But Woman never stirred. And though Nightingale flung out his chest, and fluttered his wings, and though his throat was a blur of throbbing song, Woman simply went on lying there, like a heap of clay.

'No good!' cried God. He clapped his hands and Nightingale flew startled into a bush.

As God clapped his hands, something else moved. A snake, the deadly Puff-Adder, lifted his head. He had actually been lying tucked in under Woman's side for the warmth of God's hands that was still in the clay. And now he peered over her waist, his forked tongue dancing, and said:

'I think I can solve your problem. I think I can awaken this perfect person.' And his long mouth seemed to smile.

God eyed the Puff-Adder anxiously. He didn't trust this snake at all, with its eye-chips of granite. He was almost sorry he'd made him. When he'd pressed those eyes into place one had cut his thumb, and the wound had festered for days.

'Under Woman's heart', said Puff-Adder, 'lives a Frog. It got in there with the clay you used. You didn't notice.'

God was surprised to hear that.

'I can smell it', said Puff-Adder, 'through her ribs.' And he flickered his dancing thread of a tongue over Woman's chest. 'Here it is.' He tapped with his nose to show the exact spot.

'This Frog', he went on, 'simply sucks up all the life you breathe into her. As you breathe the life in, the Frog swells up. Look.'

And it did seem to God, as he looked more closely, that Woman's stomach was slightly swollen there, under her heart.

The Puff-Adder laughed. 'Now,' he said, 'watch me extract it.'

And he began to glide up beside Woman's throat, and over her chin and was just about to slide his blunt strange head between her parted lips when God caught his tail and threw him into a stiff little thorn-bush nearby.

The Puff-Adder yelped with pain. 'You'll pay for this!' he cried. 'I would have picked that Frog out in no time. Then you could have breathed life into Woman and she would have lived. But now – now – now –'

'Well?' roared God. 'Now what?'

The snake was silent.

'I know you,' God shouted angrily. 'You'd have got in there, and eaten the Frog, if there is a Frog, and then just curled up in its place. That's what you'd have done. And you'd never have come out again. You'd have been a thousand times worse than any Frog.'

19

The Puff-Adder gave a wild laugh. Then he hissed: 'You're right. I would. But at least Woman would have come to life. And what a life! She and I together – we'd have conquered the world! We'd have driven you out among the furthest stars. Man would have crawled after us in the dust.'

God was furious. He didn't know what to think. Had the snake told the truth? Was there truly a Frog under Woman's heart? A Frog that sucked up the breath of life as he breathed it into her?

He stared at Man, lying there in a trance among the Monkeys. And he stared at the faint bulge under Woman's beautiful, lifeless ribs, and he gnawed the soft inside of his lower lip.

God advertised for help. 'Divine Rewards for whoever can make Woman live.' The creatures talked about little else. Every day, somebody came with an idea. None worked. And Woman went on lying there, perfect and lifeless.

Till one day, as God sat in his workshop, with his head in his hands, pondering this great problem, he heard a rustling voice.

A familiar voice!

He lifted his head. Whose voice was it? And what was it saying? Surely he knew that voice! Then a strange expression came over his face and his heart began to thump. He twisted round, and now he heard the voice clearly. It was coming from under a dusty heap of workshop rubbish, in that far corner.

'I can help you,' it whispered. 'I have the answer.'

In two strides he was across the room and lifting the rubbish aside, carefully, piece by piece. The dust rose and the gloom was thick. But at last he saw. He put one hand flat on the ground, and bent even lower, and peered. Yes, there she was – embedded in rubbish, like a Crab under a flat rock – his own little mother!

He'd completely forgotten her!

Gently he lifted her, and carried her out into the middle of the room. She was a great knot of doubled-up arms and legs, like a big, dry, dusty Spider. And almost weightless! He set her down, ran out and came back with a glass of brandy. She smacked her wet, blackened lips, and her eyes glittered. She smiled up at him, easing her joints slowly.

'I know your problem,' she said. She half closed her eyes, and seemed to rest a little. Then she said: 'First, bring me the new moon.'

That was easy for God. He reached down the new moon.

He watched as she half crawled over the floor, lifted the cellar hatch, and disappeared down the dark hole, with the new moon cupped in her hand. He peered after her. He'd never dared lower himself into that place. But it had always been his mother's favourite den, in the old days. And now, suddenly, her skinny hand rose up out of it again, holding the new moon like a bowl – a bowl that was brimful of dark liquid.

'Take this,' said her voice out of the darkness. 'Put it in your kiln. Just as it is. And stoke it very hot. The hotter the better.'

As God took the new moon in his hand, a little waft of fear touched him. Usually the moon was icy cold, but now it was warm. What was in it? Was it what he thought it was? He bent closely to sniff. Was it blood?

How was this going to help him?

But his mother had always known best, in spite of her oddity. So God did as he was told. Taking care not

21

to spill it, he put the new moon into his kiln. He sealed the door, and began to stoke the fire beneath. The flames roared up.

As he went on sliding logs into the blaze, God began to feel very happy. It was just like old times, when his mother was teaching him how to do things. 'The hotter the brighter the brighter the better,' he sang to himself. He almost forgot about the cold clay shape of Woman away there in the forest, and Man stretched out in a trance, under a tree, among the Monkeys. And all the time the kiln glowed brighter. Soon it seemed to be throbbing, and almost transparent, the colour of apricot, with pulsing spots of dazzling whiteness. 'Can I get it white hot?' he whispered. 'Hotter hotter brighter brighter better better –' But at that very moment the air seemed to explode in his face:

WHOOOOF–

The whole kiln had exploded and God fell over backwards with his eyebrows blown off.

And as he fell, something flashed above him, out of the explosion, like a long flame streaked with black.

He sat for a while, looking at the reeking crater where the kiln had been. Then as he got up, knocking the fiery, smouldering splinters from his hair and beard and muttering, 'Well! I'm sure that wasn't supposed to happen! What a mess!' he suddenly felt uneasy and looked round.

A strange animal stood there, watching him. A lanky, long, orange-red beast, painted from one end to the other with black stripes. Its belly and throat were frosty white. Its pelt shone. It lashed its long tail and stared into God as if it saw something moving in there.

It was like no creature he had ever seen.

But the strangest thing of all was what it held in its mouth. 'It's caught a Monkey!' was God's first thought. 'It's already started killing my Monkeys!'

But then he saw it wasn't a Monkey at all. It was a tiny Human Being! A baby Human Being!

Had this leapt out of the kiln? Was this his mother's magic? How was this going to bring Woman to life? The tiny Human Being was quite nice, but that beast was more likely to frighten her to death. No, God could see his mother's magic had got all mixed up. And now he remembered why he'd left her in the corner, and heaped the rubbish on top of her, and hired the beetles to feed her.

But the beast had turned its head. Holding the Baby high, clear of the brambles and poison ivy, it went off through the forest straight towards Woman. God began to run. He wanted to get to Woman first. But the beast began to bound. In three leaps it disappeared away ahead, in the thick jungle. Then God heard the cry of the Monkeys, and a strange, hoarse bark – not like Man at all, but God knew it was Man. And when he reached the clearing, everything had happened.

Man and the Monkeys were all together, on a high bough in the Monkeys' tree, staring down with eyes of fright. And the great beast stood over Woman's body.

As God watched, it laid the midget Human Being on Woman's stomach, stretched its own great striped length beside her, and began to lick her ear.

At once, the Baby began to stir its arms and legs. Its mouth opened like the door of a little kiln, and out of it came a thin cry.

The moment the Baby cried, the beast lifted its head and looked into Woman's face. And God, fascinated, looked at Woman's face. And the Monkeys in the tree, and Man beside them, all looked down at Woman's face. But the face remained quite still, quite lifeless.

After a while, the beast again began to lick Woman's ear gently, closing its eyes as it licked. And the wrinkled, podgy baby seemed to grow stronger, as if its cries were some kind of food. It shook its fists at the sky. It seemed to be shaking the bars of a cage.

All at once the beast leapt up and bounded away, so lightly it seemed to be weightless. And God saw it had the Baby back in its mouth. The beast stopped, sat down, and watched Woman. And the Baby hung in its mouth, silent.

God, too, watched Woman. Then he felt the hair prickle on the back of his legs. And a shiver crawled up his spine and into his hair. Woman's hand was moving. It came slowly to her head, till her fingers touched the bridge of her nose, where the Nightingale had perched with its sharp claws. She drew a deep breath and sighed.

Watching her very closely, the beast came back and laid the Baby on her thighs, and nudged it with its paw. At once the Baby opened its mouth and wailed. The air filled with its cry. And Man, too, in the Monkeys' tree, let out a cry, 'Aaaagh!' and slid down the trunk to the ground. Then he scampered across to God, and peered out from behind him. And what he saw made him cry out again: 'Aaaagh!'

Woman was sitting upright, nursing the Baby. She bent over it, her hair hanging forward like a curtain. It had happened! And the beast lay at her feet, gazing at God and Man.

God was astounded. His mother's magic had worked! But how? And what about that Frog? And

25

what about the Baby? The Baby was a brilliant idea!
Why had he never thought of it?

Wildly excited, God started forward, with Man
clinging to the fringe of his apron. But the great beast
rose to meet them. The hair on its shoulders lifted and
spread like the tail of a peacock, its jaws opened, and a
solid blast of sound hit them – a blast like the
exploding of the kiln.

Man blew away like a straw, and God reeled
stumbling after him, with his brain spinning. What
was this beast? Was it a walking kiln exploding whenever it pleased? What was it?

'Do you know what you've done?' God cried, as he
came gasping to his mother. 'Do you know what
you've let loose?' She was still squatting there on the
floor, above the cellar hatch. She grinned, showing
him all her gums, then put back her head and cackled.
Her hands, dangling over her knees, and dancing and
dithering there, reminded God of the black tongue of
the Puff-Adder.

'That,' she crowed, 'is the Tiger. He's an Angel. He
is the Protector of the Human Child.'

God was mystified. This was the first he'd ever
heard of Angels.

'Look, Mother,' he said. 'Your Tiger or Angel as you
call it – it's too much. He knocked me over with one
shout. He shows no respect. He's too frightful. The
Baby's all right. In fact, I don't mind the Baby at all.
The Baby's good. But the Tiger's overdoing it. Please
take him back.'

'Take him back?' she croaked. 'How?'

'Just take him back. If he scares me, what's he going
to do to the rest of my Creation? He's too much.'

26

His mother looked at God solemnly. 'The Human Child', she said, 'needs an Angel Protector. And the Tiger's it.'

God flew into a tantrum. 'You need a Protector,' he yelled. 'Let him protect you. My world can't handle him. He doesn't fit. If the Human Child needs a Protector, let's have something I can cope with. Something that fits.'

His mother flailed her hands loosely together – exactly, thought God, like an old Chimpanzee. 'OK!' she laughed. 'OK. I'll have him back. It's done.'

Then she clapped her palms together over her head, and held them there, fingers pointing upwards, elbows on her knees, while her face suddenly lowered and her eyes closed.

Fleeing from the Tiger's roar, Man had dived into a garbage pit. Hearing the laughter of God's mother, he'd stayed there. But now he came creeping out, and saw God returning. They went together towards Woman.

She sat as they'd left her, suckling her Baby. Man ran to her, and squatting beside her reached out to touch her hair, and gazed at her with shining eyes. The Tiger had gone.

God stood stroking his beard. He looked first at Woman, then at the Baby, then at the small, gingery, striped animal that sat beside Woman's crossed ankles, gazing at Woman and the Baby with sleepy, half-closed eyes.

This creature looked quite like a Tiger, but it was only the size of the Baby. And after one sleepy glance and one sleepy blink, it ignored God and Man.

'So what's this?' asked God abruptly, pointing to the new creature.

Woman leaned her foot over, and the little animal rubbed its ear on her big toe. She wriggled her toes, and it pressed its chin on to them, laying back its ears and closing its eyes.

'This', she said, 'is our Pusscat. We call him Tiger.'

God nodded thoughtfully. So this was how his mother had solved the problem. But at that moment the Pusscat pricked its ears. An unfamiliar sound made God look up. It seemed to come from the clouds. No, it came from the mountains.

Steep-faced mountains surrounded the forest. A horizon of mountains. They looked like giant grey or brown or blackish faces, propped up in bed with the forests pulled up under their chins, like coverlets. Out of those mountains came a strange, echoing sound. A strange, clangorous cry, rising and falling. It was like a terrible singing. A dreadful sound really.

As he listened, God felt that same shiver creeping up from his heels into his hair. Just as when Woman's hand had moved. And he knew that this was the Tiger. He frowned. And his frown became almost a grimace. The voice of the Tiger seemed to take hold of his brain and twist it.

'Tiger!' he whispered. 'Yes, Tiger!'

As he said the word, he shivered again, and felt the hair actually stir on his head.

'Tiger!' he whispered. And the same weird electrical thrill came again. He gave a little laugh.

'Tiger!' he growled. Then again, more fiercely: 'Tiger!' His eyes opened wide. He felt his hair standing up on end. And before he knew it he was roaring out: 'Tiiiigerrrr! TIIIIIgerrrrrrr! TIIIIIIIGERRRRRRRR!'

The echo of his roar came bounding and rumbling back off the mountains mingled with the appalling song of the animal. God stood there as the sounds rolled through him and over him. He had never felt anything like it. It was terrifying and yet, he had to admit it, it was wonderful. It was like nothing in his own Creation. It was wonderful in a whole new way. What was this strange new thing in his Creation?

The Tiger seemed not to have heard him. It flowed along, sometimes deep in the jungle gorges, some-times high on the rough sides where forests hung over cliffs. Its body resounded like a giant harp, as the tree shadows and the sun's rays stroked over it. A tremen-dous, invisible song, it moved slowly around the mountain circle, full of its dark ideas.

God half turned and stared at the Pusscat. It occurred to him that the Pusscat too, whether it liked it or not, was breathing that sound. And Man too. And Woman, and the Baby. Everything in his Creation was having to listen. Every creature in the thickets, every tiniest insect under the leaves, they were all breathing air that was trembling with the voice of the Tiger. Nothing could escape it. And his old mother, she was breathing it too – probably still sitting where he'd left her, with her knobbly, shrivelled hands closed over her head, and her head bowed, smiling into her closed eyelids.

The Trunk

God sometimes gets tired. But he was never so tired as the day he finished making Elephant.

'It's the last time,' he was thinking, 'the last time I make anything so big.'

In fact, he was so tired that towards the end he rushed the job a little bit. Normally he would have given Elephant a thick pelt of fur. But it dawned on him that he didn't really need this. If he slapped the clay on, and made a good, really thick skin, that would do fine. And so he whacked the special Elephant clay on in great handfuls.

At last, about four in the afternoon, the job was finished. And there stood Elephant, swinging his head from side to side, lifting first one great forefoot, then the other, and looking sideways out of his wicked little brown eye.

God was pleased. He walked all round his new creation, gazing at it from every angle. Yes, it looked pretty good. He scraped the clay from his fingers, rolled it into a tiny ball, tossed it on to his workbench, and was just about to take his apron off when Elephant screamed:

'Finish me!'

God looked round in surprise. 'You are finished,' he said. 'Away with you. Out on to the plains with you. Seize the day.'

Elephant curled his trunk high over his head and let out another scream: 'Finish me!' He twisted his tail into a tight, angry knot. 'I'm unfinished. I want a coat.'

God's heart sank. All he longed to do was sink into a hot bath. But he made his face smile.

'Dear Elephant,' he said, 'you have a coat. It's a very superior coat of real Elephant leather. It's – '

His voice was drowned by Elephant's scream: 'I want a coat of fur! You've made me wrong. Show me another bald beast.'

God could feel himself getting angry. But then he saw a tear spill from Elephant's eye, and make a black streak down to his mouth corner. He made his voice gentle: 'Elephant, I'm afraid there's none of your clay left – '

'What's that you just threw away?' shrieked Elephant. 'I saw it. You had it in your hand. That clay belonged to me. It was more me.' And his little brown eye glittered with its next tear, and swivelled and fixed on the tiny ball of clay lying on the workbench.

'But that's not enough for anything,' cried God, picking it up.

'Oh yes it is,' screamed Elephant. 'Give me some hairs. Even a few would be better than nothing. I don't want to be bald from the start.'

God sighed and patted Elephant's brow. Then very carefully he began to make bristly hairs out of that tiny bit of clay. He stuck them here and there on Elephant's head and along his back. But the clay soon ran out.

'How does it look?' asked Elephant.

'It looks', said God, 'as if you're just starting to sprout a terrific crop of bushy hair. Yes, I must say it looks pretty good. You were right to insist.'

Elephant was suddenly full of happiness. Curling

31

up his trunk, and whisking it over his bristles, he ambled off towards the plains, where the Lions glowed like heaps of crown jewels and the Gazelles drifted like shadows of clouds.

God collapsed in his chair with a gasp of relief, and gazed out into his garden. His old mother brought him a cup of tea and a bun shaped like a whelk. 'Your hands are dirty,' she muttered. 'Aren't you going to have a bath?'

But for the moment God just went on sitting there, gazing at his garden, and scraping the last Elephant clay from between his fingers and from the deep lines in his palm and from under his fingernails. He rolled it into a ball between his finger and thumb, and watched one of his Thrushes cracking open one of his Snails on the garden path. He squeezed the ball of clay flat. Then he squeezed it square. He was thinking: 'Well now, I could have made Elephant a few more hairs with this.' Then he thought about Elephant's amazing ears. And then he thought about Elephant's trunk.

God had never made a trunk before. Now that trunk was the most fascinating thing. It was a brand-new invention. He felt he'd quite like to make another, maybe smaller.

His fingers rolled the tiny piece of clay. Cleverly he shaped a trunk, with all its creases. So there it lay on his palm, a tiny trunk.

He took a sip of his tea. How if he made a really tiny Elephant? He put the trunk to his lips, to blow the nostrils through it.

Then he got a shock. The Trunk curled up, twisted and dropped from his fingers. It lay on his lap, squirming.

'Idiot!' he whispered to himself. Without thinking,

32

he'd blown life into a tiny Elephant's trunk – a tiny trunk, all on its own, without its Elephant.

'Finish me!' squealed the Trunk, writhing as if it were in pain.

God picked it up and it flailed about between his finger and thumb.

'Finish me! Where's the rest of me? Finish me!' squealed the Trunk.

It sounded like a very tiny Elephant.

God scratched his beard. The truth was, he had no more Elephant clay. At that moment, he had no more clay of any kind. Tomorrow he'd have to go out to his clay-pits and dig some fresh. But the Elephant clay was all gone. He'd used the whole lot. That's why Elephant had turned out so big.

'Just be calm,' said God. 'I'll get you some more clay tomorrow. But it won't be Elephant clay. I'm right out of Elephant clay.'

'What?' squealed the Trunk in disbelief. 'No more Elephant clay?'

'Well,' said God, 'there might be some somewhere. But it will have to be found. It's rare and precious stuff.'

'Oh no!' wailed the Trunk. 'Oh no!' It was full of Elephant thoughts, Elephant hopes, Elephant dreams, Elephant plans. Every moment, with every breath it took, it felt more and more Elephant. And the idea of creeping about without an Elephant head or body or legs was horrible.

Then God had a brainwave.

'You could help me to find some,' he said. 'You could start right away.'

'How?' sobbed the Trunk. The Trunk was actually weeping. It glistened with tears.

33

'Well,' said God, 'just go and dig anywhere. Simply dig, that's all there is to it. Start down there in the garden. As soon as you come up with the right sort of clay, I'll finish you. It won't take much.'

The Trunk lifted its end.

'There you are, start where it's soft.' And God tossed the Trunk out into his garden. Then he dropped back into his chair, sighed once, and put the whole whelk into his mouth.

The Trunk began to dig. Being Elephant flesh, it was strong. It filled itself up with whatever it found down there under the grass-roots, brought it up, disgorged it all in a pile, and called: 'How's this?'

Then away down for more.

At the end of the first day God walked in his garden in the cool of the evening, and examined the tiny spirals of earth and clay that the Trunk had brought up. The Trunk peered up at him out of its best end.

'Well,' said God thoughtfully, 'some of this we might use for insects. But none of it is Elephant clay.'

The Trunk, that had been holding itself up very straight, slumped down and lay flat.

'If you like,' said God, 'you could go on a Rat tomorrow. You'd make a very fair tail. I have a good supply of Rat clay in. I've moved on to Rats.'

'No, no!' cried the Trunk, and began to dig furiously into the earth. 'I'll find it,' it cried, 'I'll find it.'

So the days passed. And the weeks. The months, the years, the centuries. Trunk toiled away, bringing up its piles of dirt. Sometimes God looked at it, but always he shook his head sadly. And more often the

34

rain washed it away before God saw it. Or a hoof stamped it back into the soil.

But the Trunk refused to lose heart. Even though it didn't have a proper heart. 'Some day,' it cried as it burrowed among the deep stones, 'some day I shall be an Elephant. Some day I shall be whole. Some day the lands will tremble under the feet of my tribes.' And it curled itself up for joy at the very idea, and let out its trumpeting battle-cry, so fiercely that crumbs of earth fell from the ceiling of its burrow.

The Making of Parrot

In the beginning, there were even more song contests than there are now. All the creatures were just finding their voices for the first time. They were quite amazed at the sounds that came out of their mouths.

'Listen, listen to me! Listen, listen, listen to me!' they were crying. Each one wanted all the others to listen. Wolves yelled, Toads quacked, Nightingales gurgled, Alligators honked, and the Leopard made a noise like somebody sawing a table in half.

'Listen to me,' roared the Leopard. 'Oh, Oh, listen to my song! Oh, Oh, it makes me giddy with joy! Just listen!' And he went on, sawing away. It sounded wonderful to him.

But nobody was listening. Every other creature was too busy singing – head back, mouth wide, tonsils dancing. The din was terrific.

At least, it was so till the Parrot began. But at Parrot's first note, all the creatures fell silent. The Demons under the earth fell silent. The Angels in the air fell silent. And the Parrot sang on alone. Even the trees listened, breathless, to the glorious voice of the Parrot.

What a voice! Where had he come from? Who was this astounding person?

Man had just been persuading Woman to marry him. He was rubbing her whole body with coconut oil, so she glistened like a great eel. 'Marry me,' he said, 'and I'll do this to you every day.'

'Well,' she said, 'maybe.'

She loved being rubbed with oil, but what did Man mean by marriage? That was a new word. 'Marry?' What did it mean? She wasn't so sure she liked the sound of it. But she didn't want him to stop rubbing her with oil. So she said: 'Well, maybe.'

And that was the moment the Parrot began to sing.

Man stood up. Like somebody in a trance, he walked straight out through the door. He simply left Woman lying there, as if he had forgotten she existed.

'Hey!' cried Woman. 'Come back. You haven't finished.'

But Man was already outside, gazing amazed at the Parrot.

And the surrounding trees of the forest were loaded with birds of every kind, all gazing amazed at the Parrot. And in the lower branches of the trees, and between the trunks of the trees, all the kinds of animals were jammed together, in a great circle, gazing amazed at the Parrot.

Parrot surely was something to gaze at. He was actually a Dinosaur – but a truly beautiful specimen. He didn't look like a modern parrot. He was much bigger. He was quite a lot bigger than a Peacock. Nearly as big as Woman. And he was thickly covered with every-coloured feathers. These feathers didn't lie down smooth, like the feathers on the neck of a Hen. They ruffled out, like the feathers on the neck of a Fighting Cock. He looked like a gigantic Red-Indian head-dress. His face was a huge flower of rainbow feathers. His legs and feet were thick with glossy feathers, that changed colour as he stamped about. All his body was fluorescent, and as he sang, taking deep breaths, and flinging out the great flame-feathers of his wings, he seemed to be lit from inside by pulsing strobe lights – red, then orange, then yellow, then green, then blue, then indigo, then purple – then a blinding white flash and back to red. Really magnificent! And all the time, his incredible song poured out.

What a song! The crowding creatures couldn't believe it. It seemed to pick them up bodily. Their eyes boggled, their jaws dropped, and they felt like puppets being jerked by strings.

Man stared in delight. This was something new. What singing! What a marvel!

'Can you believe it? Just listen to it!' he shouted, turning to Woman, who was now leaning in the doorway, looking out sulkily. 'Can you believe it?' Man almost screeched with excitement.

Woman frowned. She just went on leaning there, feeling dull. What was the matter with her? All the creatures of the earth were there, swooning at the singing of the Parrot. And there was Man, who was so clever at everything, standing overpowered by the voice of that bird. 'What's so wonderful about it?' she kept thinking. 'Why don't I like it? What's wrong with me? Maybe my ears are funny.'

She did try quite hard to like the Parrot's song. She didn't want to be left out. She closed her eyes, and listened so fiercely her head began to ache. But it was no good. She simply couldn't like it.

But now Man was dancing around the Parrot, flinging up his arms and legs. 'I can't believe it!' he screeched. 'I can't believe it! This is ecstasy! Where have you been? Oh! Oh!'

39

That first evening, Man took Parrot into his house.
And until late in the night, the creatures all stayed
where they were, crowded around Man's house,
hearing Parrot's great song coming from inside. The
house seemed to tremble and jerk with the power of it.
And every now and again they would hear Man cry:

'Fantastic! Another! Another!'

Man was so delighted by his new friend that he
invited Parrot to live with him for ever. 'I'll supply all
you need,' he promised. 'Whatever food you like.
Shelter from the bad weather. And you can sleep in
that bed.'

'Which bed?' cried Woman. She was already fed up
with this gigantic bird. Her head was splitting with his
pounding songs. Man hadn't even looked at her for
the last eight hours. And now –

'That bed there,' said Man.

'My bed?' she gasped.

'Why not?' asked Man. He had already drunk a lot
of beer.

Woman choked. She was so furious she couldn't
speak.

'And give our new friend another glass of beer,' said
Man.

Parrot stared at her. He could see very clearly that
this Woman didn't like him one bit. But that didn't
worry him. He ruffled his feathers. The crest on his
head stood up straight, and his eyes, big and round
and cold and deadly, like a Dinosaur's, stared at her.

'Don't think you can hypnotize me, you horrible
Turkey,' shouted Woman.

'Do as you're told,' snapped the Parrot.

Man laughed and drained his glass. 'More beer for
his Lordship,' he said. 'And for me too.'

Woman went to fill the beer-jug, but she was thinking what Parrot would look like with all his feathers plucked off. Behind her, once again, Parrot burst into song and the jug in her hand began to vibrate.

Next morning, all the contestants for the great song contest were ready very early, outside Man's house, and the crowd was even bigger than usual. The Fox and the Turtle were bustling about, taking bets. Some of the creatures were terrible gamblers.

Today, most people thought Lion would win. He had never entered before. He had been out there on the resounding plains, perfecting his mighty song, for years, and rumours had been coming in. 'It's simply stunning,' said the Zebra. 'Knocks your head off,' said the Gnu. Everybody could see, by the way he lay there, eyes nearly closed, one forepaw laid over the other, that he was confident of winning.

Beside him the Wart-hog sat looking very nervous, twitching his ears and tail, occasionally shaking his head. Nobody had the slightest idea what to expect from him.

But next in line was the Giraffe. The general opinion was that Giraffe had no voice at all – she was simply dumb. Even so, the Burrow Owls put their bets on her. 'She's not dumb,' they said. 'You people are the dumb ones, thinking she's dumb.'

There were three others: a Cormorant, a Woodpecker and a Loon. Loon was thought to be pretty good.

At last, Man came out, scratching his head and yawning. Parrot emerged, and stood beside him. He looked as fresh as a giant firework in full blaze.

Usually, Man judged the singing at these contests.

But now he spoke to the crowd. 'You all heard Parrot singing last night,' he said. 'Never have I heard singing like it. We must all admit, he's in a class of his own. And so, today, I've asked him to be our Judge.'

A Monkey clapped.

'Let's begin,' said Parrot. 'Cormorant first.'

The Cormorant had been persuaded to enter by the Seagulls. He opened his beak, flapped his scraggy wings, and began.

'Aaaaaaaaaaark!' he croaked, and stopped.

'Is that all?' asked Parrot, blinking his pebble eyes.

'No, that's only the beginning,' said the Cormorant.

'OK,' said Parrot. 'Sing it to the end.'

Cormorant stretched up his neck, shifted his feet, and croaked: 'Aaaaaaaaaaark!' and stopped. 'That's the end,' he said.

Parrot stared at him.

'Next,' he said. 'Woodpecker.'

Woodpecker set back his head and laughed. After three or four laughs he stopped, and peered at Parrot. 'That's mine,' he said.

Parrot blinked. 'Loon,' he said.

The Loon writhed. His long neck performed like a snake with the itch, then shot up straight, as his beak opened.

A howling mad laugh twisted out. A Wren fainted and Man felt a shiver go up his back. Woman poked her head out through the doorway, round-eyed.

Parrot nodded and smiled. 'Giraffe,' he said.

Giraffe swayed. What looked like a bubble travelled slowly up her neck. Giraffe opened her mouth, and after about six seconds burped.

A baby Chimpanzee turned a somersault and

42

screeched, till its mother hit it.

'Is that your song?' asked Man. Giraffe nodded gracefully, and lowered her thick, long eyelashes.

'Wart-hog,' said Parrot.

The Wart-hog's performance was quite good. He whirled on the spot, fell on his back, threshed his legs, churned with his tusks, writhed and contorted in a cloud of dust, and all the time let out noises like a cement-mixer. At last he stood up panting. He was sure he'd won.

'Lion,' said Parrot sharply.

Lion stretched, yawned, took a deep breath, then suddenly gripped the earth with his claws and roared. The blast knocked off several rows of birds, and Man grabbed the rail of his veranda. Parrot's feathers flattened for a moment, and all the baby animals began to cry till their mothers hushed them. Then everybody waited.

Parrot seemed to be thinking. Then he said: 'The result of this contest is – Winner: ME!'

The Lion frowned. All the animals began to chatter. 'How is that?' roared a voice. It was Lioness. 'How can that be? How can you be winner?'

'Because –' said Parrot. And suddenly he burst into song. He leaped out into the middle of the beasts. His feathers flamed and shook, his colours throbbed. His voice was not only utterly astounding, it was amazingly loud. Man shouted with delight:

'He's right. He's the winner!'

And Man began to clap. All the animals began to clap. And when Man began to dance, they all began to dance. Clapping they danced, and dancing they clapped, while the Parrot whirled and sang.

But Lion, Giraffe, Wart-hog and Loon stood apart in

43

a group. 'He's not a bird,' said the Loon. 'He's a lunatic!'

'I might have won!' snorted Wart-hog. 'I was in there with a fighting chance!'

And Lion said: 'Something will have to be done about this fellow.'

But Giraffe stuck her head in through a side-window in Man's house, and saw Woman lying on the floor, weeping.

'Your husband has gone crackers,' said the Giraffe. 'It's that Parrot.'

Woman looked up. 'I'm leaving,' she sobbed. 'I've had enough. That Parrot is a monster. Have you seen its eyes? And is that supposed to be singing? It's made me deaf.'

She began to push things into a suitcase. 'Man was going to marry me,' she cried. 'Since that Parrot came he never even looks at me. The Parrot orders me about and I sleep on the floor. I'm off.'

'Wait,' said the Giraffe. 'We have a plan.'

It was true. The Giraffe may have been a dumb singer, but she was a clever planner.

'Wait till we come back,' said the Giraffe. 'Give us two days.'

Woman sat on the bed weeping. She nodded wearily: 'OK, OK. But two days is the limit.'

The Giraffe, the Loon, the Lion and the Wart-hog went to God. They told him that Man was getting married to Woman and that he wanted God to be there. But he daren't ask. He was too modest. In fact, Man was a little bit afraid of God. So the animals had come to ask what Man didn't dare to ask.

'I'd like very much to come to that wedding,' said

God. 'Woman is my favourite invention.'

'But what he really wants,' said Giraffe, 'is for you to sing a song.'

'What,' asked God, 'at the wedding?'

And Loon said: 'Woman thinks that if you sing at her wedding, they will be happy ever after. She believes that. She's praying you'll come.'

God laughed. 'Simple!' he said. 'No problem. When?'

'Tomorrow,' growled the Lion.

The animals came to Woman, and explained their plan. 'The wedding must be tomorrow,' they told her. 'And you must get that Parrot to sing.' So the same night, when Parrot was fast asleep in Woman's bed, a great heap of glowing feathers, Woman got up from the dirt floor where she slept with the cat, and whispered to Man:

'You begged me to marry you, do you remember?'

He woke up and lay staring into the dark.

'What's that?' he said. He thought he was dreaming Woman's voice. So she said it again: 'You begged me to marry you, do you remember? Did you mean it?'

'Yes!' he said. 'Oh yes. If you will, I'll rub you every day with warm oil. Oh yes! Will you? Will you?'

'Tomorrow,' she whispered.

He would have jumped out of bed for joy, but remembered the Parrot and lay silent. Then he said: 'I'm sorry about the Parrot. But you know how I need music. I get carried away.'

'If he'll sing at our wedding,' she said, 'I will try to like him.'

By dawn, the news of the wedding had spread. The

animals assembled from every corner of the forest and plains.

'What's this about a wedding?' cried Parrot, rushing back into the house. Man was already draped with honeysuckle, and he was rubbing Woman's body with warm oil. 'It's our wedding day,' said Woman. 'Will you sing for us? Can you sing a Marriage Song?'

'Haha!' laughed Parrot. His eyes seemed to whirl, but they were actually darting to and fro. His feathers were a-tremble. 'Sing a Marriage Song?' he cried. 'Only give me the chance!'

'Oh, I knew you would, Parroty,' she cried, and flinging her arms round him she covered his feathers with oil.

As he stood at the river's edge, trying to wash the oil off, Giraffe came strolling up.

'Hello, Parrot,' she said. 'I expect you're looking forward to hearing the new singer.'

Parrot blinked. 'New singer?' he asked. 'What new singer?'

'At the wedding,' said Giraffe. 'He's supposed to be simply the best ever. They say he's already here. Some animals persuaded him to come. I think Man was hoping you'd sing. It's going to be a mix-up. I expect it will end up with both of you singing.'

Giraffe sauntered off, and Parrot glared after her. He was beginning to feel angrier and angrier. First, he was furious about the oil on his feathers. And twice as furious about this new singer butting in on his show. A new singer? The best ever?

Parrot knew what he'd do. He'd challenge this new singer to a Marriage Song contest, on the spot. And he'd flatten him. He'd just crush him with his Parrot Song-power. The poor fellow wouldn't even be able to croak.

47

So Parrot shook himself like a great, gaudy dog, and came up from the river raging with eagerness to challenge the new singer.

God arrived looking like a beggar. He told nobody he was God and nobody recognized him. He merely said he'd heard there was going to be a wedding, so he'd brought a present. It was a hive full of bees. Man had never seen such a thing.

Already the creatures were crushing tightly around Man's house. And Parrot stood there on the veranda, staring hard at the Beggar. Could this be the new singer? He didn't look like much competition, if he was.

Man was impatient to start. But this was the first wedding ever, and nobody knew how to do it. Then the Beggar had a bright idea. He smeared Man's and Woman's faces with honey, from the hive. Then Man licked Woman's face and Woman licked Man's face, and when all the sticky sweetness was gone – that was it, they were Man and Wife. So simple!

'And now sing a song,' roared the Lion.

The Beggar nodded and smiled. But before he could open his mouth, a bellowing shout came from the veranda: 'Wait!'

All creatures looked at the Parrot. And as they looked at him, Parrot began to sing.

But from the first moment something was wrong. Something was stuck in Parrot's throat. He stretched his beak wide open, his feathers rippled and flared, his colours throbbed – but he choked. Finally he coughed and spat out – a Fly. A big Bluefly.

It buzzed on to the veranda rail, and sat there, cleaning the back of its neck. The Beggar nodded and smiled.

Parrot began again, but he'd hardly got into full voice

48

before the same thing happened again – another Fly, which joined the first.

Parrot braced himself in rage, and began again. His voice choked, grated, strangled, as he forced out his song – and Fly after Fly shot out, till the veranda rail was crawling with them, and Parrot's eyes were blood-red.

He gagged finally, and bent over, coughing drily – while Fly after Fly came whizzing out of his mouth.

'Perhaps while we're waiting,' said the Beggar, 'I could sing a little song.'

And the Beggar began to sing. As he sang, the animals seemed to grow in size. Woman began to pant and cry. And Man too, he suddenly collapsed to his knees, and crouched there, his elbows on the ground, clutching the top of his head. And out of the ground all round flowers began to push up and open. Huge blossoms and tiny florets. And out of every twig in the forest clusters of blossoms burst and hung down. And out of the core of every flower unfolded a different Butterfly. And Butterfly after Butterfly came out of the flowers, just as Fly after Fly had come out of Parrot's mouth, till the air was full of Butterflies, that settled everywhere on the birds and animals and covered Man and Woman like a rich, quivering cloak.

Then the Beggar began to sing more strongly. And now Parrot seemed to clear his throat and let out a screech. He was trying to sing. Everybody could see he was trying to sing, but all that came out were not Flies now but more and more horrible screeches. And as he screeched he writhed. It was truly awful to watch him. His feathers now seemed to be real flames, devouring themselves. And the Beggar stepped towards him with his eyes shining and sang a great torrent of song straight at Parrot. The poor bird whirled and blazed and screeched, while his feathers scattered like burning embers from a kicked bonfire, and his body shrank. He was like a whirling Parrot being tossed, or maybe a Parrot being bounced on the end of an elastic.

Suddenly Woman ran forward. She ran fearlessly into the blast of the Beggar's song, and caught up the Parrot, and ran into the house with it, and silence fell.

When Man uncovered his eyes and looked up, he saw the incredible garden of blossoms and Butterflies. The Beggar had disappeared. Man went into the house looking for his new wife, and found her nursing the Parrot.

He could only just recognize the bird. It was no bigger than a small Monkey. Its feet were scorched, scaly twigs. Its face was a bent lump, like glass that had melted and hardened again. Its eyes were little marbles in ashen sockets. Only a few colours. Only a few feathers. And its voice – its voice was just the burned-out wreck of its song.

'Poor Parrot,' said Woman. 'Poor little Parrot!'

But gazing at the Parrot all Man could think about was the tremendous song of the Beggar.

The Invaders

In the deep darkness, God suddenly raised his head, and listened.

What was that? Was it a voice?

He strained his ears, listening into the silence.

Whatever it was, it had wakened him up. The silence was thick, as if made of dense leaves.

All through the world, just like God, the creatures listened. Some that had been sleeping had jerked awake. Their eyes bulged, wide and moist in the pitch black, as they listened. Some that had been creeping froze – with one paw lifted. Their ears craned.

All were listening. All were astonished. It had been a new noise, like nothing before.

And though it hadn't been very loud, every ear had heard it, all over the earth, at the same moment.

As if it had come from the inside.

And now, as they listened, and just as those creeping creatures were thinking of putting their lifted paw silently down, the sound came again.

It was a voice. It was words. It said:

'I am taking over.'

It didn't come from inside. It came from far out in space. But from everywhere in space at the same time. A peculiar, hoarse, quiet, howling voice. How can a howl be quiet? But it was. It was a sort of howling whisper. Or a whisper, a harsh, thin whisper, with a howl far away down inside it. Very eerie!

All creatures on earth looked straight up into space to see what it might be. That night was starless. Their gaze disappeared into complete black.

God at his window stared up into the perfect black. And again the voice came, louder, and as if angrier:

'I am taking over the earth. All creatures shall be my slaves and food. God shall be my slave. I am coming to enslave the earth. I am coming to enslave and devour you all.'

A terrific silence followed. God's skin had tightened with goose-pimples, and his hair was trying to stand on end, struggling in its matted curls.

Who was this? What was this? A voice from beyond? And what else?

Had he made the earth too beautiful? Had he made all its creatures too beautiful? Had he attracted the greed of some space-being – some horror, perhaps? It sounded as if he had, and it was coming.

And as he stood there at the open window he heard the little cries of fear beginning, whimperings, cater-waulings, whinings, screeches, moanings, chitterings, snufflings, roarings, wailings, mooings, bleatings – all the voices together, a sea of sounds that grew louder and wilder. Till the whole earth was crying out. He listened in dismay. What could he do? That voice from space had terrified the whole earth. Panic was begin-ning. A sounder of Wild Pigs went plunging through his gooseberry bushes, barking and squealing. A great Horse was churning to and fro on his lawn. He could hear it in the dark, whinnying and grunting and whining and shaking its nostrils. He could imagine its staring, frenzied eyes, its mane on end, its tail-stump stuck straight up and the long tail flaring from it, as it whirled about in terror. Foolish Horse!

He cupped his hands to his mouth and bellowed with all his strength:

'Quiet out there! Quiet! There's no reason for alarm. Have no fear. God is here! It's a false alarm!'

That sound too was heard all over the earth. But it travelled slowly. Like waves widening from a rock dropped in a pond, it swept around the globe.

Hearing it, the creatures became quiet. Was God going to make a speech? Was he going to explain? Was he going to make it all right?

Soon the whole earth was silent once more, listening now for God. And God was thinking: 'I'll just give them a few comforting words,' when that other voice came again.

So all the creatures, listening in silence for God's words, heard instead that horrible, howling, scree-ching whisper from space, from the very stars, it seemed to be, but from all the stars together, from every hidden star at the same time. And it said:

'I am coming. Listen, O slaves. I am your new Master and I am coming. I need blood. I need food. And you, God! Hahahaha! You poor little God! You shall be my backscratcher! Hahaha!'

The voice was no longer a whisper. It sounded a whole lot nearer. And bigger. It was a bigger, fiercer voice. Just the voice, quite apart from what it said, the voice alone was terrifying. And the wild laugh made the ground shiver a little.

At once, every creature closed its eyes, opened its mouth to the limit, and emptied its lungs. From the whole earth, one great cry went out.

The din was deafening. God slammed his window

53

shut, and went groping for a candle. His fingers were trembling.

How long before sunrise? How fast was this voice approaching? It was obviously coming pretty fast. But space is big. He found his candle and lit it with a snap of his fingers.

He sat on his bed and clutched his hair, and tried to think, while outside his window the earth wailed and sobbed, and up in the darkness – what? What? God's eyes rolled upwards, and he listened.

It was a terrible dawn for the creatures. God walked out in the dew, doing what he could to calm them. All the smaller creatures tried to get into his clothes, to hide near him. Up his trousers, inside his shirt and his sleeves. And as he walked he looked like a walking bee swarm with all the birds trying to land on him for safety. The bigger animals had gathered around God's house. Even Elephant and Lion and Leopard were in a shocking state, especially their wives.

God called a meeting.

'This voice in space', he began, 'is very odd.'

All the creatures fell silent. Even the Flies landed and listened.

'Yes, it is very, very odd,' said God. 'Most peculiarly odd.'

They all gazed at him, full of trust. Surely God would know what to do. Surely he would protect them. But he simply stood there, scratching his beard and frowning and saying:

'Very, very, very odd,' and again he frowned, sternly.

Buffalo suddenly saw that God didn't know what to say. He didn't know what to do either. God was as baffled as they were. And Buffalo was just about to

54

THE INVADERS

shout: 'We ought to get ready to fight,' when the sky seemed to split.

All the creatures flattened, as if a giant hand had slapped down on them. Their eyes were squeezed tight shut, their ears flattened, their jaws clenched, as the voice came from directly overhead.

The same voice, but now very loud, like a great clangour inside a huge iron ship.

'Surrender! I call on you all to surrender. You are in my power. It's already too late to fight.'

Only God still stood upright. He lifted his fists and shook them at the morning sky, which was bright blue, a beautiful morning, with a few fluffy clouds in the west.

'Do your worst, whoever you are!' he roared. 'We're ready for you! Do your worst! We're ready!'

The answer from the skies was a long, howling laugh, and then:

'Prepare! I shall be on top of you before you know! Prepare! Countdown has begun!'

God waited. After a few minutes, when nothing happened, he roused the animals. And now, working in a fury, he began to arm all his creatures.

'Have no fear!' he called, as he fitted tusks to the Elephants. 'Go and practise with these.'

The Elephants surged off, and began to practise on big trees, levering their roots out of the ground, ripping their bark off. 'What weapons!' they cried, and blew their trumpets.

Every creature pressed towards God, crying for weapons.

The Wild Pigs stormed off, like a charge of cavalry. Their jaws had been fitted with short, hooked tusks, as sharp as razors. They slashed through a field of turnips, making the slices fly.

The Wild Bulls trotted off, knotting their tails, looking deadly under their new horns. 'We're the land rockets,' they boasted. 'When his tanks appear, watch us,' and they shook their heads, so their horns seemed to spin like propellers.

His fingers flying faster than a typist's, God fitted weapons to every creature. The Rhinoceros bounded off, in his armour-plating, tossing his long horn upwards. 'Where's the enemy?' he shouted. 'Let me topple his towers!'

'That's better!' snarled the Leopard. And he made such terrific swipes with his new bunches of claws, like clubs full of steel hooks, that some nearby tall flowers fainted and became creepers ever after.

Even the rats and mice scampered about, clashing their fangs, dying to come to grips with the enemy.

Everybody felt safer. Pretty soon they were all equipped. And all longing for the fight.

'Let me at 'em!' boomed the Bear, and he took a swing at a tree stump, which actually exploded, just as if he'd tossed a bomb into its roots.

God called his army of new warriors.

'It's no good being well armed,' he shouted, 'if we've no discipline.'

Then he showed them how to form round him in a square. The biggest and most dangerously armed creatures on the outside, the smaller and quicker creatures inside. God stood in the middle of the square. His main weapons were blinding lightning and thunderbolts. He kept in reserve earthquakes and volcanoes. He also had mists, hail the size of oranges, and tornadoes which could lift up weights bigger than Elephants and whirl them far out to sea. He had incredibly freezing winds that could refrigerate most enemies solid in about five seconds. His last resource was meteorites. He was slightly afraid of those. The damage they could do, he knew, was out of this world. But he'd practised a lot, on the moon, and knew he was pretty accurate. It was a last resort.

The creatures stood in their places, gazing upwards. God gazed upwards. The Elephants stood fast, swaying like boxers and making little lunging movements with their tusks. The Lions lifted their upper lips. The Leopards made sure their jaw muscles were loose.

But God was worried. He'd put heart into all his creatures, giving them weapons. But he still had no idea just what this enemy might be. Its voice had made him feel quite sick with anxiety. He had a feeling this was going to be some battle! He was already thinking: 'The moment it appears, up there in the sky, I'll have a go with the old meteorite, and risk it.'

Silence descended on the strange army. All gazed upwards into the blue. It actually was a gorgeous morning, fresh and light, a little wind just nodding the flowers. A Lark suddenly burst into twitterings of joy, till a Baboon slapped it and a Mongoose gave it a fierce look. They waited.

Finally, God couldn't bear to wait any longer. He cupped his hands and roared upwards into space.

'Whoever you are, you'd better go back. I advise you to turn round and go back. We're very heavily armed and perfectly prepared. Please don't be foolish. Go and try your luck with some other Creation. You haven't a hope here.'

There followed a moment's pause, then the air shook. Even the air inside their mouths and inside their lungs seemed to shake. The noise was stunning. It came from everywhere. It was no longer above in space. It was in the earth, in the trees, in the air, and even, yes, inside each other. A most tremendous shout:

'ATTAAAAAAAAAAAAAAAAAAAAAAAAACK!'

Every creature had the impression that a meteor had come rushing from nowhere and had hit them smack in the ear. On both ears. A truly shocking noise, a horrendous moment of noise!

Then came dead silence.

With clenched teeth, with wild, popping eyes, all claws out, horn-tips trembling, lips lifted from fangs, ears flattened, bodies tensed and quivering, the beasts stared at each other, waiting for IT.

God crouched, his eyes stretched very wide, to miss nothing, a meteorite at the ready, another one slowly circling his head on standby.

But still nothing happened.

A Rabbit broke down with the tension and gave a few sobs.

Gradually the creatures relaxed. They blinked, they licked their dry lips, they readjusted the positions of their tails. The Wolf glanced at God.

God's arm lowered slowly, and he straightened. A slight frown came over his brow.

Gazing round uneasily, he passed the meteorite to his left hand, pushed his right hand under his left armpit, and scratched himself.

The Wolf, as if imitating him, pointed its nose, flattened its ears, closed its eyes, and with one hind foot fiercely scratched the back of its ear.

A Cheetah, without taking its eyes off the topmost leaf of a distant tree, which had just moved the wrong way in the wind, thoughtfully lifted a hind leg and tried to scratch its belly. Then, forgetting the leaf, it sat and began to nuzzle and chew at its belly-fur savagely.

God was also scratching his belly. Then the back of his knee.

A pack of Wild Dogs began to scratch, all together, like dancers without music.

Was it catching? Was it itching powder? The densely packed square of creatures was shuddering and shaking. The Vultures fluffed their wings and burrowed in their feathers with their beaks. The Monkeys rolled on the ground, scratching fiercely, with grimacing faces. A Badger sat, teeth bared, with a blur for a hind leg. Pigs squirmed on their backs, trying to find sharp stones or twigs to scratch them.

The whole army was shuddering in a disorderly heap. Every animal and bird was scratching itself, or scratching its neighbour, or trying to do both.

And then God, scratching his belly, found what felt like a speck of grit. It twitched between his finger and thumb as he squeezed it. It was alive.

He peered at it. A tiny bushy face peered out at him, with two ferocious red eyes. The mouth opened, and that same tremendous voice came out:

'Surrender! You are overpowered!'

And the tiny thing leaped into his beard.

God began to laugh.

'It's a Flea,' he cried. 'We've been invaded by Fleas!'

He scratched and laughed wildly. He seemed to be tickling himself. And all the creatures began to laugh and rake at their itches. And itching they scratched. And scratching they laughed. And laughing they itched and scratched and laughed and scratched and itched and laughed and scratched and scratched –

They scattered through the woods, rubbing themselves against trees and rocks, scratching and laughing, and itching and laughing, and scratching and scratching –

God went into his house for a bath.

The Snag

Right from the beginning Eel was grey. And his wife was grey. And his children were grey.

They lived in the bed of the river under a stone. There they lay, loosely folded together, Eel and his wife, and two of his children. They breathed, and they waited, under a big stone.

Eel could peer out. He saw the water insects skittering about over the gravel, and sometimes swimming up through the water, to disappear through a ring of ripples. Where did they go?

He saw the bellies of the Trout, the Dace, the Minnows, and one Salmon, hovering in the current, or resting on the points of the stones on the river-bed, their fins astir endlessly.

All day he lay under the dark stone.

But at night, when the sun went behind the wood, and the river grew suddenly dark, he slipped out. His wife and his two children followed him. Their noses were keener than any Dog's. They could smell every insect. They rootled in the gravel of the river-pool, nipping up the insects.

But wherever he went over the river-bed, he heard the cry: 'Here comes the grey snake! Look out for the grey snake! The grey snake is out! Watch for your babies!'

The fish could see him. Even in the dark, the fish

with their luminous eyes could see him very well. They darted close, to see him better.

'Here he is!' piped a Trout, in a thin treble voice. 'He's coming upstream. Horrible eyes is coming upstream.'

And then: 'Here he is!' chattered the Minnows. 'He's turning back downstream.'

Wherever he moved, the fish kept up their cries: 'Here's the grey snake now. Here he comes! Watch your babies!'

Eel pretended not to care. He poked his nose under the pebbles, picking out the insects. But the endless pestering got on his nerves. And his two children were frightened. 'We're not snakes,' he would shout. 'We may be grey, but we're fish.'

Then all the fish began to laugh, so the river-pool shook. 'Fish are silver,' they cried. 'Or green, or gold, or speckled, with pinky fins. Fish are beautiful. Fish have scales. They are shaped like fish. But you are grey. You have no scales. And you are a snake. Snake! Snake! Snake!'

They would begin to chant it all together, opening and closing their mouths. And Eel and his wife and children would finally glide back under their stone and lie hidden.

In a few minutes the fish would forget about them.

If there had been anywhere else to go, Eel would have gone there, to escape the fish of that pool. Once he did take his wife downstream, to a much bigger, deeper pool. But that was worse. Nearly thirty big Salmon lay there, as well as many Trout and Dace and Minnows. The Salmon had shattering voices. They were used to calling to each other out on the stormy high seas. And now when Eel came slithering from under his stone, when night fell, a deafening chorus met him:

'Here comes the grey snake. Here he comes to eat your children. Here he comes. Watch out!'

And all the time he was hunting they kept it up: 'Go home, grey snake! Go home, grey snake!'

Finally Eel led his family back to the smaller pool, where there was only one Salmon.

His two children stopped going out at night. They lay curled up under the stone, crying. 'What are we?' they sobbed. 'Are we really grey snakes? If we aren't fish, what are we?'

Eel scowled and tried to comfort them. But he couldn't help worrying. 'What if I am a grey snake, after all? How can I prove I'm a fish?'

Eel had only one friend, a Lamprey. Lamprey was quite like Eel, but he was so ugly he didn't worry about anything. 'I know I'm a horror,' he would say. 'But so what? Being ugly makes you smart.'

One day this Lamprey said to Eel: 'I know a Fortune-teller. She could tell you what you are. Why don't you ask her?'

Eel reared up like a Swan. 'A Fortune-teller,' he cried. 'Why didn't you tell me?'

'I've told you,' said Lamprey.

This Fortune-teller, it turned out, was the new moon. 'How can the new moon tell fortunes?' asked Eel.

'She tells fortunes only for a few minutes each day,' explained Lamprey. 'You have to get to her just as she touches the sea's edge, going down. Then she tells fortunes until she sinks out of sight. You have to listen very carefully. You don't hear her with your ears. You hear her with your thoughts.'

'Let's go,' said Eel. And he wanted to set off that minute downstream, but Lamprey checked him.

'Take a witness,' said Lamprey.

'A witness?' asked Eel. 'What for?'

'Unless you have a witness to what the new moon says, the fish will never believe you. Take the Salmon.'

The Salmon was so sure the new moon would tell Eel he was really a snake, and not a fish at all, that he was eager to come. 'I want to hear that,' he cried. 'I'll bring the truth back. Then you can stay out there in the sea, you needn't come back at all. It's the truth we want, not you.'

So they set off. It was quite a journey, getting to the new moon. But finally Eel got there, with Lamprey beside him, to keep his spirits up, and, skulking behind, the Salmon.

The new moon was actually a smile without a face. It lay on the sea's rim like a face on a pillow. And the Smile smiled as Eel told his problem. It smiled as it sank slowly.

'You are a fish,' said the Smile. 'Not only are you a fish. You are a fish that God made for himself. God made you for himself.'

'Me?' cried Eel. 'God made me for himself? Why?'

'Because,' said the Smile, 'you are the sweetest of all the fish.'

The Salmon slammed the water with his tail. He'd always thought he was the sweetest. This was bad news on top of bad news.

'Say that again,' cried the Eel.

'You are the sweetest of all the fish,' said the Smile.

It spoke so loud the whole sea chimed like a gong, with the words.

Eel didn't know what to say. 'Thank you,' he stammered. 'Oh, thank you.' He was thinking how his children would jump up and down, as much they could under their rock, when he told them this.

'But,' said the Smile, as it sank. It seemed to be sinking faster and faster. There was only a little horn of light left, a little bright thorn, sticking above the sea.

'But?' cried the Eel. 'But what?'

'There's a snag,' said the Smile, and vanished.

'What snag? What's the snag?' cried Eel.

But the Smile had gone. The sea looked darker and colder. A shoal of Flying Fish burst upwards with a shivering laugh, and splashed back in again.

Still, Eel had what he wanted. And both Lamprey and Salmon were witnesses. Salmon had already gone, furious, as Eel and Lamprey set off home.

Back in the pool, Eel called all the fish together and told them exactly what had been said. 'I am a fish,' he said. 'Not only that, I am God's favourite fish. God made me for himself. Because among all the fish, I am the sweetest.'

'It is true,' said the Lamprey. 'I was there.'

'Yes,' said the Salmon. 'Perhaps she did say that. But what did she mean? That's what I'd like to know, what did she mean?'

Even so, the fish were impressed. They didn't like it, but they were impressed. And from that moment, Eel and his wife and children surged about the pool throughout the day as well as the night. 'Make way for God's own fish,' he would shout, and butt the Salmon. 'Make way for the sweetest!'

The fish didn't know what to do. The story soon got

about. The Heron and the Kingfisher told it to the birds. The Otter told it to the animals. A crowd of them came to Man, and told him what had happened.

Man, who was drinking very sour cider, which he had just made out of crab-apples, pondered.

'What', he said finally, 'does the Eel mean by sweetest? How sweetest? Sweetest what? Sweetest nature?'

All the creatures became thoughtful. Then they became wildly excited.

'Man's got it!' they cried. 'What does the horrible Eel mean by sweetest? Sweetest how?'

The fish came crowding around Eel and his family. 'Sweetest what?' they shouted. 'How are you sweetest? Come and prove you're the sweetest! You and your hideous infants. You and your goblin wife.'

'It's a riddle,' said the Salmon. 'The new moon posed a riddle. What does sweetest mean?'

'We are sweeter than any Eel,' cried the flowers. And the wild roses and the honeysuckles poured their perfumes over the river.

'And we are sweeter than any dumb Eel,' cried the Thrushes, the Blackbirds, the Robins, the Wrens, and they poured out their brilliant songs over the river.

'And my children are the sweetest of all the animals,' cried the Otter, holding up its kittens. 'They are not,' cried the Sheep, and she butted forward her two Lambs. 'No, they are not,' cried the Fox, suddenly standing there with a woolly cub.

'Among the fish,' cried the Eel. 'That's what she said. I am the sweetest among the fish. Who cares about perfumes? Who wants to smell? And who cares about song? What counts is the thought. And who cares about fluffy darlings? The Otter grows up to

68

murder Eels. The Lamb grows up to butcher the flowers. The Fox-cub grows up to murder the Mice. What sort of sweetness is that? No. My sweetness is the real sweetness, the sort that God loves best.'

'Taste?' asked Man. 'That leaves only taste.'

Eel would have blinked, if he had had eyelids. Taste? He hadn't thought of that.

'That's it!' shouted the fish, sticking their heads out of the water. 'Taste! Cook us and eat us, see who's the sweetest. Taste us all. Taste us all!'

Eel felt suddenly afraid. Who was going to taste him? Was Man going to cook him? But the fish were shouting to Man: 'You can eat one of each of us. And then eat Eel as well, and then you can judge. Here we are. Here we are.'

The fish were quite ready to let one of each kind of them be eaten so long as it meant that Eel too would be eaten.

'No,' cried Eel. 'Wait.'

But fish were jumping ashore. One Trout, one Dace, one Minnow, and even that Salmon – he too was offering himself. All to get the Eel killed and eaten!

Eel twisted round and fled. But the Otter plunged in after him. And in the swirling chase, the Otter grabbed Eel's wife. She was much bigger than Eel anyway.

Eel coiled under the stone with his two children. He couldn't believe it. The oven was glowing, the fish were frying. And his wife too! It was terrible! But all he could do was stare and feel helpless.

And Man and Woman were already testing, with dainty forks and thin slices of buttered brown bread.

They didn't like Dace at all. He tasted of mud. The Minnow was quite nice – but peculiar. The Trout was fairly good – but a little too watery. He needed lemon and – and – something. And the Salmon – the Salmon, now! Well, the Salmon seemed just about the most wonderful thing possible – till they tasted Eel.

Woman uttered a cry and almost dropped her fork. Tears came into her eyes and she stared at Man.

'Was there ever anything so delicious!' she gasped. 'So sweet! So sweet!'

Man rested his brow on his hand.

'How have we lived so long,' he said, 'and not realized what gorgeous goodies lay down there, under the river-stones? How could anything be sweeter than this Eel?'

'Eel!' he shouted. 'You have won. God is right again. You are the sweetest!'

Eel heard and trembled. And he shrank back under the stone, deeper into the dark, when he heard Man say: 'Bring me another!'

Otter came swirling down through the current. Otter was working for Man. Eel and his two children shot downstream. But one had to be hindmost. One of the children. And when Eel looked round, only one of his children was following.

And as they slipped and squirmed down through the shallows, among the stones, towards the next pool below, the Heron peered down out of heaven and – Szwack! The other Eel-child was twisting in the Heron's long bill. The Heron too was working for Man.

But the Eels were so sweet, neither Otter nor Heron could resist eating them on the spot. From that moment, the Otter hid from Man and spent all his time hunting more Eels – for himself. And from that moment Heron was afraid of Man – flapping up and reeling away with a panicky 'Aaaark' – only to land somewhere else where he could go on hunting Eels –

for himself. Neither Otter nor Heron wanted to hand over what they caught – Eels were much too sweet!

But Eel himself hid from all of them. He oiled his body, to make it hard to grip. And whenever he sees the slightest glow of light he hides deeper under the stones, or deeper into the mud. He thinks it is Man searching for him. Or he thinks it is the point of the moon sinking and he suddenly remembers THE SNAG.

Yes, the snag.

The Playmate

'I want a playmate,' said Woman.

Man stopped, turned and stared at her. Here he was, his food-gathering bag on a stick over his shoulder, and his club, to defend himself from the hoodlums among the animals, stuck in his belt, ready to tramp all day searching for tasty mushrooms, and honey, and edible snails, and all she wanted to do was play.

'A playmate?' he echoed. 'Can't you weave another carpet? They're very pretty.'

'I've woven twenty-eight. They're seven deep on the floor. I'm sick of carpets.'

'Then – make a pot,' suggested Man. 'You're a very good potter. I love your pots.'

'I'm sick of pots,' she cried.

'Then weave a basket.'

'I've woven baskets till – look! My finger-ends are raw. If you mention baskets again I'll scream.'

She sat on the bed, looking miserable. Man's heart sank.

'What happened to the pet rat?' he asked. 'He was good fun.'

'He bit me, didn't he,' she shouted.

'Be calm, be calm!' said Man. He knew he'd have to do something. But what?

'Ask God,' she said. 'Tell him if I don't get a play-mate, I'm off.'

72

'Off?' cried Man. 'Where to?'

'Just off,' she shrieked. 'Off! Off! Off! Flap! Flap! Flap! Like a bird! Go and get myself eaten by Lions. Find some excitement. Anything. I'm withering inside!'

She was growing more and more agitated.

Man tried to calm her. 'I'll ask him,' he said. 'Today. A playmate, you say.'

He was just about to go when he turned back. 'What kind?' he asked.

'How am I to know?' she yelled. 'It's God's job – thinking things up. All I've got is a snake. It sleeps the whole time. I'm perishing of boredom and snake-sleep!'

Man set off. His day was ruined. It wasn't always so easy, getting a word with God. First of all, it wasn't so easy to find him.

But today he was lucky. Man found God kneeling in a forest clearing. He seemed to be pressing his ear to the ground. But then Man saw he had his right arm buried to the shoulder in some sort of hole. He strolled up.

'Lost something?' he asked casually.

God frowned, rolled his eyes and twisted his mouth. He was obviously groping for something down there, deep in the earth. Then he gasped and straightened up. His hand came up out of the hole and God laughed. Between his fingers something struggled.

'There we are,' he said, and laid the creature on his palm. It took a few wriggly steps, then peered at Man over the edge of God's forefinger, a tiny froggy face, with brilliant jewel eyes.

73

'A Newt!' said God. 'Funny. I simply had a feeling about it. I knew there was something down there. But I'd no idea – ! Well, well, well!'

'Is he your latest?' asked Man.

'Hard to say,' God replied, peering into the Newt's eyes. 'He might have been here a while. Some things take an awful lot of work. But others – they just seem to turn up, somehow. All ready-made. Very odd!'

'Maybe somebody else is making them too,' suggested Man, getting interested. But God turned angry eyes on him, and stared at him, and so Man said quickly: 'Actually, I have a request. For a special kind of creature.'

Now it was God's turn to be interested. 'Really? A special creature, eh? How special?'

'My wife needs a playmate,' said Man. 'She says she wants some excitement.'

God's eyes became grave. He lowered the Newt on to a lily leaf in a swampy pond. He pushed the lily leaf under the surface, with one finger, and the Newt floated off. Then, laying its arms and legs close to its sides, it wriggled away downwards into the gloom, like a dart with ribbons.

God sat back on his heels, and gazed at Man. 'An exciting playmate for Woman!' He nodded thoughtfully. 'Well,' he said, 'I already have one or two ideas. How soon?'

'Tonight, maybe?' said Man. 'Suppertime, about?'

'OK,' said God. 'Tonight.' And he stood up and strode away, his head bowed in thought.

Man licked his lips nervously. He would have liked to say a little bit more. He would have liked to say: 'Something not too big, not too noisy, not too wild.' But God had gone. Man began to gather frilly orange mushrooms, pausing now and again. What he didn't want God to do, was make another Man.

That evening Man and Woman ate their supper in silence. As the sun set, the glow of the fire seemed to grow brighter. Man could feel himself becoming more and more anxious. His wife wasn't angry, and she wasn't exactly sulking. If anything, she was just sad.

'Well,' he said at last, 'your playmate's coming this evening.'

She looked up, with round eyes, but said nothing.

'God didn't exactly say what sort,' Man went on. 'Only we can be sure it will – do the trick.'

Woman blinked and gazed into the fire. Man thought she looked a little bit less unhappy, so he felt happier. He told her about the Newt. All she said was:

'I hope it isn't going to be a Newt.'

They sat on, waiting. Wolf began to howl. Bats began to snatch Moths from the edges of the fire's little flames. But still no playmate. Finally they went to bed. Man couldn't sleep. Was God going to fail him? Or maybe the playmate had already arrived, and they hadn't noticed. Maybe it was a Moth. Or a Bat. These didn't seem like very good playmates. But then, thought Man, God had some funny ideas. Not all were what you might call perfect.

The moon rose full and shone into the room. Man closed his eyes and tried to force the morning to come. Maybe in the morning –

But suddenly, he knew his wife beside him had lifted her head off the pillow. He opened his eyes and listened.

Something was coming through the forest, towards the house. And not very quietly either. Branches cracked and broke.

'Ooooh!' his wife whimpered.

Man got out of bed. Some of the animals did not like him too much. His hand found his club in the dark. He waited, standing in the middle of the room, as the crashing came closer.

And now he heard celery stalks snapping in the garden, and a crunching and a munching.

Was it an Elephant? The chomping noises came still closer. Now the thing was standing just outside the door, slurping and chewing and breathing hard.

Very gently, Man pulled the door tightly closed and slid the big wooden bar-bolt into its sockets.

At the same moment something pounded on the door. The whole house shook slightly, and a mouse screamed.

'Who's there?' shouted Man.

Dead silence answered him. Then the breathing started again, with gasps and grunts as the door creaked. Something was trying to force a lever or maybe tusks into the edge of the door. Man swung his club and slammed that spot with all his strength. A screech of pain went up, and a heavy creature thudded away. More screeches followed, then whinings, and finally silence. Man and Woman waited, hardly daring to breathe, straining their ears.

Suddenly a dark shape appeared at the window and Woman screamed. A huge bulk blocked the moonlight. It was coming in.

Again, with all his strength Man whirled his club, and after a few thuds and more screeches the dark thing fell away from the window, and the moon looked in as before.

Man stood panting, waiting for the next attack. His

wife crouched behind his knees, sobbing.

Suddenly, to his amazement, the whole house began to rock. He had built it on low pillars, and now something seemed to have got under it, and to be hoisting up one corner.

A groaning series of gasps came from under the floor, as the house reared higher. Man and Woman crashed to the back wall and the whole house toppled over. They struggled under a heap of pots and carpets and baskets.

They were hardly clear when the house began to heave up again and with another groaning gasp toppled right over on to its roof. Now Man and Woman were lying on the ceiling, which had become the floor, and on top of them were all the pots, baskets, carpets, and the bed too.

'Don't worry,' shouted Man, 'I built this house to last.'

But already it was toppling again. And again. And again. And the dreadful groaning gasps outside had become a sort of laugh. And the house was trundling over like a giant, creaky crate. And Man and Woman and all their possessions were tumbling inside it like clothes inside a washing machine. And the terrible creature, whatever it was, kept on heaving it over, like some sort of toy, with horrible grunty laughs.

Inside, Man and Woman dived and rolled, bruised and dizzy, in a hail of broken crockery, in a great writhing tangle of carpets. There was nothing to cling on to. Man kept trying to push his wife out through the window, but she screamed and clung to him. 'Don't throw me to that monster,' she cried. So then he tried to climb out while he carried her. But each time, before he could get more than his leg over the sill, the house heaved up and crashed over, and there came another gibbering laugh from somewhere out in the dark, and they were both in a heap under their furniture.

At the end of the garden, the ground sloped steeply to the river. And finally it happened. After toppling the house to and fro, and round and round and about, the powerful mystery beast rolled the house to the top of the sloping bank and down it went. Kerrash! Kerr-rrack! Kerrrash! Kerrrackity! Splooooonge!

Water poured in through the window and the loosened joints, and Man and Woman heard the wild laugh rise to crazy shrieks. Their dark prison rocked gently and the water deepened.

Man pulled his wife out through the window. They sat on the roof with a Snake and a Mouse. Their half-sunk house was floating in mid-river, revolving slowly. The sky over the forest was pink with dawn. And they could just make out, in the pinky-grey light, a black massive creature leaping up and down on their garden, at the top of the slope, turning somersaults and shrieking, waving immense, long arms.

God rescued them, and their house, and brought them back home. He just couldn't understand it. 'But I made him specially as an exciting playmate!' he said. 'He only wanted to play.'

'With our house?' cried Man. 'He thought we were a squarish sort of ball. He bounced us about all night.'

'Still,' said God, 'he was only playing. He just wanted you to play.'

They found a gigantic black hairy ape, asleep among the remains of the melon patch, worn out with his fierce all-night game. Woman gazed down at the creature in horror.

'It's only a Gorilla,' said God mildly. 'He's really very sweet.'

'That thing a playmate for me?' she gasped, and she cringed close to Man. He put his arm round her as she began to sob again.

'You'll have to take it back, God,' he said. 'It won't do. You can see it won't.'

So God sent Gorilla off into the forest, and thought again. He asked Woman: 'What sort of playmate do you want? I thought you wanted excitement?'

She gazed dreamily down the river. They were sitting at the end of the garden, at the top of the slope. Man was away finding food.

'Like the sea,' she said at last. 'The beautiful sea!'

The sea was a blue haze, beyond the headlands at the mouth of the river. God gnawed his thumbnail.

'Like the sea!' he pondered. 'How like the sea?'

'Beautiful – like the sea,' she said.

'So,' said God. 'A beautiful friend. I thought you wanted an exciting one.'

'Beautiful,' she said. 'And exciting.'

God gazed at her. She smiled at him, hazily.

'Right,' he said. 'I'll have another go. But this time, you help.'

He sat Woman on the dunes, at the top of the beach, and walked down towards the sea's edge.

'Now,' he called, 'give me some sort of hint.'

They both stared at the sea. And suddenly:

'There!' she shouted. 'Look! Like that. Oh, lovely!'

A great green comber was heaving up, a long hollow wall of glassy green. Full of lights and weedy rags, it reared and reared, higher and steeper, as it raced towards them. Its top burst into flower, the foam began to topple towards them, spilling down its face.

'Lovely!' shouted Woman, and her voice was lost as the whole colossal cliff of water collapsed, exploding in foam, and the beach shook. Long arms of boiling milk froth shot up the sands and piled around God's ankles.

He nodded. 'I think I've got it.' And with those words, he ran at the sea, dived into the face of the next great comber, and disappeared.

For a long time Woman waited, watching the breakers. The tide was coming in. The wind blew off the land, so the white bursting crests of the breakers flamed over their backs.

Then she noticed a white commotion out at sea. She thought it must be a great fish fighting at the surface. Then she saw God, sitting astride something silver and glistery. He vanished, in an eruption of foam. But he re-emerged, much closer. He was racing towards the land. He was astride something, a racing bulge under the surface of the sea. And as he rode up into the breakers a huge shaggy head reared out of the water ahead of him. She saw its deep-sea staring eyes. It reared a long neck, draped with seaweed. She watched in horror. It was bigger than Elephant. Then its shoulders heaved up, and as the great comber burst around it, it turned. She saw its long side, like a giant white-silver shark. For a moment, it seemed to writhe and melt, as if it were itself exploding into foam, and the next thing God was rolling up the beach, battered by foam.

He got up and looked towards her, waved, then ran again into the sea, diving like a seal under the next comber.

Soon she saw it again, that struggling out at sea. And once more, God was riding towards the beach. He seemed to be riding in the crest of one of the towering combers of surf. But she saw he was having a problem.

And again she saw the shaggy head lifted, and an arching body with God astride it. In a smother and welter of foam, uptossing spray, and amid the earth-shaking thunder of the breaking surf, this time God rode up the beach on the back of some animal. She saw it now, nothing like so big as a whale, or a whale-shark. It tried to turn and go back into the combers, as the foam sucked back into the undertow. But God forced it to go on up the beach. It wheeled to left and to right but he forced it ahead.

And so it came, tossing its head and lifting its knees high as if it only wanted to go backward or maybe straight up into the air. Its whole body seemed to be tossing and quivering.

God rode it up on to dry sand and right to the dunes. There he dismounted. And the beast stood, glistening, shivering and snorting. A dazzling smoke seemed to rise off it. God had tied a thick sinew of kelp weed-stem round its nose, and that seemed to hold it. At any moment Woman expected to see it melt and spill foaming away down the sand into the sea. Instead, it reared and surged and stamped. It was bursting with fierceness, as if a whole sea were somehow packed inside it. Glaring pulses of dazzle seemed to come out of it, like flashes off the sea. Its skin quivered and rippled like the skin of a blown wave. Woman stared, dumbfounded, thrilled and frightened.

'What is it?' she shouted, over the sea's hoarse, constant roar. 'It's gorgeous!'

'It's a She,' said God. 'Not an It.' And then he reached out, and before she knew what he was doing he took hold of her long hair, and sheared through it with his thumbnail, as if he were plucking a flower. Woman clasped her cropped head. Then she watched as God laid one hank of her hair over the creature's neck, and one great bunch of it he coiled round the creature's stumpy tail, and let it trail and flow.

At once the beast became quieter. It seemed to change. It looked at Woman, its ears pricked up, its nostrils opened wide. It stepped towards her and gently sniffed her face. She could feel the power-waves coming off it, so that her skin prickled.

And suddenly Woman had the strangest feeling. Part of her was there, lifting in the wind, on the creature's neck and tail, like its own banner. And she felt the beast was part of her.

'She's me!' she shouted excitedly. 'I can feel she's me!'

It was a completely new feeling. It twisted in her, making her want to leap and run.

'Up you get,' said God, and he set her astride the strange animal. He slapped its rump.

'Away home, Horse,' he shouted.

It surged forward, it bounded over the dunes. She hung on to its neck. It knew the way. It ran as if it floated. Some of the sea's sound came with it.

And so, as Man set down his bag of mushrooms and nuts and sweet roots and snails and whelks and loganberries, he heard a drumming. And as he looked up, a great glare of light seemed to burst over him, and this strange, silvery beast swirled to a stop in front of him, as if a flame had blazed up out of the earth, and now stood there, flaming and trembling, waiting for a command. To his amazement, his wife jumped down, out of the dazzle.

'What's this?' was all he could gasp.

'Just what I wanted,' she said. 'My new playmate. God calls it Horse.'

So it was, the playmate God had created for her. And so it still is. And Man has learned, whenever Woman grows sad, she is missing her Horse.

The Shawl of the Beauty
of the World

God rubbed his eyes and yawned. His candle blinked. Out through the open doorway, in the dark blue sky, a star blinked.

It was late. Again he yawned. As he yawned, a thin squirt of juice from somewhere at the back of his throat sprayed over what he was making.

Straight away, the creature-shape squirmed. He held it tight.

'Now then!' he said sternly. 'You're not finished. Don't start living yet.'

But the thing squirmed again. The juice from the back of God's yawn had somehow brought it to life.

It was a funny-looking object. Just like a Turkey all plucked and ready for the oven. Even its head was pink and bare. And it had no legs.

God felt cross. If this thing had come to life, he really would have to finish it. He'd wanted to go to bed and finish it in the morning. Was it really alive? It had become still again. God shook it carefully. It lay still.

He wondered if he dare leave it. He stood up, walked to the door of his bedroom, taking the candle. He stood there awhile, watching the dark lump on the workbench. It lay still.

So God went to bed, and left the strange creature as it was, unfinished.

Early next morning, God was awakened by a wild banging at his door. It was Elephant's wife. Elephant had fallen into a crevasse. God called his old mother up, and set her in a rocking-chair, to keep watch over his unfinished creature, still there on his bench. Then he took his ropes and started off, to rescue Elephant.

As the sun rose, Man's two children, Boy and Girl, came peeping in through the door of God's workshop. They saw God's grizzle-haired old mother asleep in the chair. They saw the plucked Turkey shape on the bench. They tiptoed in.

Boy took the creature cautiously by the sharp beak. He lifted its head, on its long limp neck.

'Wake up, baldy!' he said, and gave it a little shake.

The creature opened its eye and blinked. Boy let go of the beak and stepped back. But the head didn't just drop on a limp neck on to the bench. Instead, it craned up. And now the head was looking at its own bare body and the stumps of its no legs. It certainly was wide awake.

'Oh!' cried Girl. 'Poor thing! Oh you poor thing!'

The creature burst into sobs. At least, it would have burst into sobs if it had had a voice. It gaped its beak and gasped, but nothing came out. Only tears bulged from its eyes and dropped on to its own goose-pimpled chest. It felt terrible. And suddenly it wanted to shout terrible things. It wanted to shout: 'Where are my legs?' And: 'Where are my feathers?' And: 'Why am I only half made?' And: 'Why me?'

But no matter how much it stretched its mouth, and strained its lungs, not a sound would come out.

And now it wanted to yell: 'And no voice either! Where is my voice?'

It writhed and heaved and squirmed on the bench,

and rowed at the air with its stumps.

'Oh!' cried Girl, and began to cry, watching the Poor Thing's efforts. Then she looked round and saw two clawed feet, bundled together, lying on the end of the bench.

'These must be meant for you,' she cried, and began to loosen the chain that was wound and knotted tightly round the ankles of the two scaly, clawed feet. They did look like a bird's feet, but they were actually the feet of a Demon. That was another story. And God had bound the feet in this fine but very strong chain because though they no longer grew on the Demon, they were still full of devilish tricks. And he'd laid them there in full view, on the end of the bench, so he could keep an eye on them.

Now Girl stuck each foot in place on the Poor Thing's stumps, and with lightning devilish power they took root. They clenched and unclenched. And suddenly, with a heave, the creature rolled off the bench and flailing its naked wing-stumps landed on its new feet, on the floor, with a thud.

It took three steps, then put back its head, opened its beak and – nothing came out.

'Find a voice for it,' cried Girl. But Boy had already found a small bottle. He peered at the label, and spelled out: 'Voice of Voices.'

'Is this creature called Voices?' he asked.

Girl snatched the bottle, opened it, opened the Poor Thing's beak and upended the bottle. A brilliant, heavy, green vapour poured down the Poor Thing's throat.

It blinked. It felt, all at once, that it no longer existed. It closed its eyes, and saw all the stars. But all the stars, in a funny way, were inside itself. All space was inside itself!

Then it opened its eyes and saw Girl again gazing with her large brown eyes, and Boy behind her, and the old woman crumpled in the rocking-chair. And out through the door it saw the red rising sun.

Then the Poor Thing's beak opened and out came the most tremendous yell: 'WOOOWWW!'

God's mother jumped straight out of the chair on to the bench. Boy's hair stood on end. Girl fainted.

And where Poor Thing had stood was nothing. Poor Thing had vanished. And at that moment the room went dark.

God's figure blocked the doorway. He was panting. 'What did I hear?' he bellowed. 'What's happened?'

What had happened was this – at that dreadful yell from the Poor Thing's new voice, the Demon Feet had been frightened out of their wits. And they had simply fled! And they had taken the Poor Thing with them – new voice and all.

And as the Feet scampered through the woods, and through the swamps, whenever the Poor Thing tried to cry, 'Oh, please stop,' out came that dreadful yell again:

'WOOOWWW!'

And away the Feet went, more terrified than ever.

And as they went, out came that yell, again and again: 'WOOOOWWW! WWOOOOW!' And 'WHAAAAAAAAAAOW!'

'It's nearly got me!' thought the Feet. 'Oh! Oh! I'm done for! Oh! Oh!'

And they leaped into a thorn-bush, and the yell came again:

'WAAAAAAOW!'

And the Feet leaped over a cliff, thinking: 'It will never dare follow me.'

But straight away, right on top of them, the yell came again, out of the beak that was fastened to the neck that was fastened to the body that was fastened to the legs and the Demon Feet:

'WAAAAAAAAOW!'

Then the Feet ran into a black burrow and straight away the yell came deafening in the blackness of the hole:

'WOW!'

And the Feet thought: 'Help! It's in here with me!' And they shot out of that hole and ran and ran till the Poor Thing collapsed exhausted on a sandy plain.

All the creatures gathered around it and began to laugh. Poor Thing didn't dare utter a sound for fear his Demon Feet should start running again.

But all on their own, the Feet began to caper about. They began to dance. They leaped and twirled. And of course, since they were growing on the end of the Poor Thing's legs the Poor Thing leaped and twirled, whether it liked it or not. Stark naked, flapping its foolish naked wing-stumps, it leaped and twirled.

The animals laughed harder than ever. And the Demon Feet were just thinking 'Why are those creatures laughing? Don't they appreciate a Demon Dance? I'll kick sand in their eyes if they don't stop laughing.' But at that moment the Poor Thing couldn't stand any more, and it shouted: 'I can't help it!'

But all that came out was a dreadful:

'WAAAOW!'

In a cloud of dust, a scatter of pebbles, the animals fled.

But the Feet stood. This time they didn't flee. It had suddenly dawned on them where the voice came from. And now they wanted to laugh. Yes, the Feet laughed. And:

'WOW! WOW! WOW!' yelled the Poor Thing –
though actually that was the Demon Feet laughing.
'WAAAAAOW! WOW! WOW!'

Then the Feet set off after the fleeing animals. In no
time, they overtook the Wart-hogs:
'WOW!' they yelled, and the poor Wart-hogs almost
died with fright. They scattered, they jammed their
heads down holes and under the roots of trees.
Now the Demon Feet raced on, and overtook the Gnus:
'WAAAOW!' yelled the Feet. And the Poor Thing
just could not do a thing about it. When the Feet ran,
and the Feet yelled, the Poor Thing had to run and
yell. And now the Gnus tried to scatter. But they fell in
heaps, their gangly long legs tied in knots, and the
Demon Feet laughed madly, at the top of their voice:
'WOW! WOW! WOW!'

The Feet were enjoying themselves all right. And so
they raced on. And wherever they found an animal,
that animal saw this stark naked Turkey creature hurt-
ling towards it out of the distance, right up close, and
then heard that ear-splitting:
'WAAAAAOW!'
Some animals went white with shock, instantly.
Some simply fell stunned. Some plunged into lakes.
And what did the Poor Thing think about it? The
Poor Thing was helpless, in the power of the Demon
Feet. The Poor Thing didn't know what to do. The
Poor Thing simply rolled its eyes, as the Feet rushed it
towards yet another poor animal, and as it felt its beak
being forced open from the inside, and the terrible
voice getting ready to blast out, it thought: 'Oh no! Not
again! Not again!'

But it couldn't stop it. And out it would come:
'WAAAAAAAAAAOW!'

And the poor animal had to hear it. And it might be only a tiny shrew that actually died on the spot.

Suddenly – a flurry of darkness in the air, and Crow landed just in front of the Poor Thing.

'God', said Crow, 'is looking for you. He wants to give you your feathers. You do realize, I hope, that you are featherless, stark naked, and an embarrassment to the birds.'

The Demon Feet became still. They listened, through the Poor Thing's ears. And the Poor Thing too, of course, listened.

'Well, feathers would be very nice,' it was thinking. And suddenly it felt excited. Perhaps they were pretty feathers. Some of the birds were gorgeous, though not Crow. And so the Poor Thing cried: 'Oh please! Oh yes! Oh please!' But all that came out was a terrific:
'WAAAAAAAAAAAAAAAAAOW!'

Crow closed his eyes, as a cat does when you blow in its face, and gripped the earth with his feet.

'OK,' he said. 'Come to God at once.'

The Demon Feet needed no urging. In no time, the Poor Thing arrived at God's workshop. But God was out in the hills, the coat of feathers draped over one arm, looking for it.

God's mother saw it, peering about. 'There you are,' she cried. 'Oh, I am sorry. It was all my fault. Oh, I'll never forgive myself!'

The Poor Thing stared at this old lady who stood wringing her hands and screwing up her face in the strangest way. It kept its beak tightly shut.

'If only I'd stayed awake,' she went on, 'Man's little brats would never have given you the wrong feet and the wrong voice.'

The Poor Thing blinked. And the Demon Feet listened. What was this about wrong feet? They suddenly remembered the chain that had bound them so tightly.

'And now it's too late,' wailed God's mother. 'I saw these spare funny-looking feet, and I thought they were mistakes or leftovers. I threw them to the Fox. He ate them. And they were your feet. Oh! Oh!'

She was actually weeping. The Demon Feet crimped slightly, as they tried to smile.

'And your voice,' sobbed the old lady. 'Your charming voice! Oh, it was so pretty! My Magpie stole it. He fed it to his baby Magpies. Oh! Oh! God was so furious!'

She mopped her eyes with the edge of her shawl.

'But I want to make amends,' she said finally. 'I want to give you something.'

And now she laid in front of the Poor Thing the most astounding robe. It was blue, but inside the blue every other colour raced and glimmered. It was green, but inside the green every fiery colour flared and throbbed.

'God made it for me,' said the old lady. 'He called it the Peacock, which means: the shawl of the beauty of the world. He said: "Mother, my most beautiful creation is for you." But now I want you to have it. And wear it. Oh please. Please, please accept it!'

The Poor Thing couldn't believe its eyes or its ears. The Demon Feet were aghast with amazement and joy.

Trembling, like somebody stepping carefully under

93

a freezing waterfall, the Poor Thing put on the robe.

Behind it, the long train swept, full of eyes like coloured moons racing through their changes. It lifted the train and spread it, and it was like a whole heaven full of big, darkly blazing planets spinning in their rings.

God's mother clapped her hands with delight.

'WAAAAAAAOW!' yelled the Poor Thing and the Demon Feet together.

Then the Demon Feet leaped, and danced a few steps. Then they and the Poor Thing together stamped and danced in a circle, shuddering the great lifted spread of feather heaven and all the suns and moons and planets. A tall, fine crown shuddered on the Poor Thing's head.

'WAAAOW!' it cried. 'WAAAAAAOW! WAAAAAAAAAAAAAAAAAAAAAAAOW!'

And God's old mother stamped and danced with him, and clapped her wrinkled old hands, and yelled:

'WOW! WOW! WOW!'

And God appeared. A short, rather dowdy brown, tasselled drape of feathers dropped from his hand. He stood amazed at what he saw. Then he began to laugh. He too clapped his hands.

'The Peacock!' he cried, and he laughed till his tears ran down. And he breathed to himself:

'Wow!'

Leftovers

At the end of his working day, God usually had a few bits and pieces left over. Sometimes, just to clear up his worktable, he would stick these together and make a funny-looking mixture of a creature. Then he would breathe life into it.

The creatures he made in this way felt very mixed up. They had a hard time knowing how to carry on. 'What am I?' asked the Okapi. 'Am I a Giraffe? Or a Bushbuck? Or a Zebra? Or what?' He hid in dark forest, trying to work out what he was. But he would never work it out. He had been mixed up by God.

One day God felt he ought to give his workshop a spring-clean. He set to. It was amazing what ragged bits and pieces came out from under his workbench, as he swept. Beginnings of creatures, bits that looked useful but had seemed wrong, ideas that he'd mislaid and forgotten. He stared at the pile of odds and ends. There were off-cuts and waste scraps of bad weather, which was his very latest invention, only just completed. And bits of the flowers from long, long ago. There was even a tiny lump of sun.

He scratched his head. What could be done with all this rubbish? At that moment he smelt sausages. His mother was cooking his dinner. Suddenly he felt ravenous. It had been a hard day. So now, in a great hurry, he mixed the whole heap of sweepings together, squeezed it into shape, breathed life into it, and set it down on the edge of the plains. 'There we are,' he said. 'Run off and play.'

As God let go of it, the creature lifted its head, and opened its mouth. What it wanted to say was: 'Give me a sausage!' Because it too felt ravenous. A little bit of God's hunger for the sausages had got in there, along with all the other scraps. But what came out of it was a long roll of thunder. God stared at his new animal in alarm. But then he laughed. He'd noticed a bushy clump of blue-black cloud among the sweepings. It must have been a piece of thunder cloud. He hoped there were no lightnings or thunderbolts in it. Still, it couldn't be helped. So he laughed and called: 'Not bad for leftovers!' and went off to chomp his sausages.

The creature shook himself. He felt very uncomfortable. He blinked. There was something terribly bright behind his eyes. He did not know it, but that was a chunk of the sun – just a leftover scrap. He wrinkled his face and shook his head. Then he lowered his nose and again a long roll of thunder came out of him. All the creatures of the plains lifted their heads with question marks in their eyes.

But he was thinking: 'So I am Leftovers, am I? Made out of the scraps. Made out of the bits that couldn't be fitted into anything else.'

And as he thought this he became more and more angry. And that little bit of God's hunger in him made it worse. Again he shook his dazzled head and let out another roll of thunder. 'God made all his other creatures with great care and with great love,' he said to himself. 'But me – he just screwed me into shape like a ball of waste paper, and dropped me on to the earth as if he were throwing me away! Aaaaaah!' And he thundered again. 'I am rubbish!' he thundered. 'I am Leftovers.' Thunder after thunder rolled out of him. And at every roll of thunder he grew more and more bitter. He was working himself up.

'If I had God here now,' he rumbled, 'I'd swat him like a Fly! I'd splat him to a splodge! I'd swallow him alive and howling! Yes! Yes! Revenge!' he thundered. 'Revenge!'

A Wild Cow standing nearby stared at him. 'Shame on you,' she cried. 'You scruffy-looking ruffian. Go and get yourself washed. Go and get yourself combed.'

Leftovers glared. Then, before he knew what he was doing, he rolled out a great crash of thunder, soared through the air and landed on top of the Wild Cow. 'Help!' she cried, as her legs crumpled. She thought heaven had fallen.

All the animals watched horrified as Leftovers killed her and ate her. This was new!

They came trotting closer, twitching their tails and flicking their ears. The Gazelles stamped. The Wild Bull pawed up clods of dirt. He couldn't believe what had happened, but it was beginning to sink in. The Elephants lifted their trunks.

'You can't do that,' squealed the Elephants. 'You should eat leaves and twigs.'

'That's not done,' brayed the Zebra. 'You should eat grass.'

'Eat flowers,' bleated the Gazelles.

'I shall tell God,' bellowed the Wild Bull. 'You shall be punished. God will not like this. I shall have justice!'

But Leftovers seemed not to understand them. He

thought he'd just eaten a wonderful pile of sausages. He watched them through his eye-pupils that looked like tiny keyholes. He licked his lips. Then he yawned.

The animals became more and more excited. 'Eat flowers! Eat grass! Eat leaves! Not the Wild Cow! Not the Wild Cow! We shall tell God. Now you'll be punished.'

But they all kept their distance. There was something in his yellow dazzled eyes they did not like. And none of them wanted to end up like the Wild Cow.

Then, to their amazement, he laid his head on his paw and fell asleep, right there among the bloody bones of the Wild Cow. The animals were enraged. In a great mob, they turned and rushed off over the plains, to tell God.

'He's a cannibal!' squealed the Elephants.

'He's a gluttonous, ghastly, ghoulish ogre!' bleated the Bonteboks.

'He's a big, bad, bloodthirsty bandit!' bleated the Blesbok.

'He's a scruffianly, ruffianly, rag-bag hooligan!' bleated the Springboks.

'God will punish him!' bellowed the Wild Bull.

And they milled around on the hilltop, raising a red cloud of dust, stretching their necks up, or their trunks, and crying:

'Oh God, you've made a mistake! Do you know what you've done? Leftovers is killing our wives! Help! Help! Take him back! Take him back! Leftovers is killing our wives!'

And the Wild Bull humped his shoulders and bellowed: 'Justice! I demand justice from God!'

God could not hear the animals, but he could see them, leaping and churning about in the dust-cloud.

He thought they were dancing to celebrate their happiness and the beauty of the earth. He nodded in Heaven. And to show them that he understood, he stirred the top of a thundercloud with his right hand and let a roll of thunder rumble out across the horizons.

When they heard that, they scattered in terror. They did not know it was God's new toy, which pleased him almost more than anything he had created so far.

'A giant Leftovers in Heaven!' they cried. 'He'll fall out of the sky on top of us, just as Leftovers dropped on the Wild Cow. It must be his unborn brother!'

God frowned and stopped chewing for a moment. 'Funny!' he muttered. 'What's got into them?'

But from that moment all the animals were afraid of Leftovers and his titanic brother in Heaven. And from that moment too the Wild Bull began to follow him, peering out from the deep thickets of thorn and watching him, waiting for the moment of revenge.

Leftovers was uncontrollable. Every third day, the craving for sausages, that hunger of God, came over him and would not let him rest. It drove him over the rocky ridges, slouching from thorn-bush to thorn-bush. He truly was a scruffy-looking object, like an old tatty blanket draped over a broken-down sofa. His face looked like a giant, battered, dried sunflower. The animals would have laughed at him if it hadn't been for the rolls of thunder that came pouring out of his mouth, and the way he would suddenly stop, and stare through his deadly keyholes. Then they knew what to expect. Next thing, some fat happy animal would suddenly let out a honk, and collapse, as if struck by lightning. And that would be Leftovers, lying on top of it.

And when his skin was stretched as tight as a huge sausage, he'd roll on to his back and sleep, frowning over the lump of sun behind his eyebrows. Then he looked exactly like a bursting sackful of rags, till his skin began to slacken a little, and once again the hunger of God woke him up.

Meanwhile, every day, the Wild Bull's rage grew worse. He slammed his horns into an Ant-hill, and tossed the lumps about, to strengthen his neck. 'God cannot feel my grief,' he bellowed. 'God cannot hear us.'

The animals tried to calm him down. 'You mustn't take justice into your own hands,' cried the Tree-Shrew. 'That's bad. Be patient. Leave Leftovers to God. God will punish him.'

But the Wild Bull crashed his horns into the trunk of a baobab tree, to toughen his brains. 'I can't wait for God,' he bellowed. 'I shall deal with Leftovers alone.'

The animals were horrified. If Wild Bull started fighting, where would it end? 'God must be told,' squeaked the Meerkat. 'And soon.'

At last a Weasel managed to get to God, and gave him the whole story. God slapped his brow. He remembered Leftovers. But where had those eating habits come from? God had forgotten how his mother had been frying sausages, and how he had breathed life into Leftovers with breath full of craving for sizzling sausages, out of a mouth watering at the very idea of sausages. But he felt it must be his fault somehow. He came hurrying down to earth, very upset. Was he really to blame for Leftovers' horrible behaviour?

All the animals gathered around God, to tell him how Leftovers was killing their grandmothers and grandfathers, and their wives and their children.

'Leave it to me,' said God at last. 'Just leave it to me.'

He found Leftovers licking his paws. 'Do you realize,' he said very sternly, 'what you're doing?'

Leftovers gazed at God. He'd just eaten so much he could not get up. He blinked.

'You can't carry on like this,' said God. 'This – well, it's murder, isn't it?'

Leftovers yawned.

'Do you hear me?' roared God, and he slapped a couple of thunderclouds. Lightning plunged into lakes and forests.

'It's no good shouting at me,' said Leftovers mildly. 'You made me. I am what I am. And that's all there is to it.'

'I am what I am!' screeched God. He sounded like an Almighty Elephant, and he shook his thunderclouds like separate fists. Lightnings spattered the sky.

The animals crouched on the plains. 'They're at it now,' cried the Hare. 'Leftovers must have sent for his brother. Somebody'll be hurt now! Oh boy!'

'I'm your fault,' said Leftovers quietly.

'My fault?' gasped God. He was nearly speechless at Leftovers' insolence.

'You shouldn't have made me of rubbish. I'm rubbish, aren't I? What do you expect from rubbish? I can't help it. Now go away.'

And while God stood there, Leftovers laid his head on his paw and fell asleep.

God sat on a stone, thinking. What could he do? Leftovers was right. God shouldn't have made him so carelessly. He should never have let that little bit of thundercloud get into him, for one thing. But where had that hunger come from? Because that was the dreadful part, the hunger.

As he sat there thinking, Man came strolling up.

'There's a very easy answer to your problem,' said Man.

'There's a reward,' said God, 'for the right answer.'

'Listen to this,' said Man. 'Leftovers is bitter because you made him of rubbish. Isn't that true? He's taking his revenge on your Creation. Killing the animals.'

'So it seems,' said God.

'So all you need to do', said Man, 'is make him King of the animals.'

God gave a little laugh, and raised one eyebrow.

'A King has to protect his subjects, doesn't he?' said Man. 'Instead of being rubbish, an outcast on the earth, he'll be King. He'll be your representative over the animals. He'll become good. He'll stop being bitter. He'll feel so good, he won't need to take any more revenge. It will change him.'

'What about that hunger of his?' asked God. 'Will that change too?'

'Oh, that!' said Man. 'Well, you could always feed him on your sausages.'

God liked this idea. He called all the animals together and explained his plan. But all they did was stare at him, saying nothing. None of them trusted Leftovers.

'We'll put a crown on him now, while he's asleep,' explained God. 'And when he wakes up, you all kneel and say: "Greetings, O King!" And you, Hyena, will say: "And here, O Your Mighty Majesty, are God's own sausages for your royal breakfast." I'll supply some. Then while he's eating I'll come by and talk to him.'

The animals looked fearful.

'What if he doesn't believe us?' bleated a Sheep.

'If the crown's on his head. And the sausages are there sizzling. And you all act your parts. He'll believe it,' said God.

They all thought hard how they would act. But they still weren't sure.

Then the Fox cried:

'King Leftovers doesn't sound right. That name Leftovers will remind him. That will set his thunder rolling. That will bring the lightning out of the ends of his great paws. He needs a new name.'

God thought. He didn't like wasting anything. 'If we knock a few letters out of his name, we could call him Love.'

'No,' bellowed the Wild Bull. 'He's a convicted murderer, remember. I do not forget the past. You're letting him get away with it. I'm having nothing to do with this.' And he plunged away into the dense thorns.

'Very well,' said God. 'How about Leo?'

So they agreed. And God produced a crown from his treasury in Heaven. It was actually a small-scale model of the Zodiac. The sausages were prepared. And when Leftovers awoke, he was greeted by all the animals kneeling and touching the ground with their foreheads.

'Greetings, O Mighty King,' they cried. 'Greetings, O Mighty King Leo!'

And Hyena crawled forward, pushing a huge plate of hot sausages in front of him. 'O Mighty King Leo,' he chanted. 'O representative of God among the animals, here is your royal breakfast, hot from Heaven.'

Leftovers looked around. He was puzzled. But there was no denying the sausages. And now he saw them, he knew they were exactly what he had always wanted. And as he tasted the first, he closed his eyes in bliss. This was the taste he was always searching for. Heavenly sausages!

Hyena spoke: 'Your Majesty, you have forgotten to hand your crown to me.'

'Crown?' asked Leftovers.

'While you eat your royal breakfast, I always polish your royal crown, given to you by God,' said Hyena.

Then Leftovers noticed the weight on his head. He took off the crown and gazed at the shining gold and at the jewels in seven different colours. He pretended not to be surprised, as he handed it to Hyena, who began to polish it with his little tail.

'Of course,' said Leftovers. 'It slipped my mind.'

'Blessings on his Mighty Majesty King Leo!' yelled a Baboon.

And all the animals, in one great voice, shouted: 'Blessings on his Mighty Majesty King Leo!' And the Elephants stood in a row and blew a majestic fanfare, as Leftovers ate his sausages.

As he ate he thought: 'Am I me or am I Leftovers?' But he couldn't answer. He really couldn't tell. 'It seems,' he thought, 'that I dreamed I was a ragged, nasty creature roaming about in the thorns, murdering my subjects and eating them!' He shuddered with horror, and picked up another sausage.

And as he munched he thought: 'This is the life!'

At that moment God came strolling by.

'Good morning, King Leo,' God greeted him. 'How is the kingdom of the animals? Is everybody happy?'

'Indeed,' said King Leo, speaking in a slow, dignified way, 'my subjects are all happy.'

'It must be thanks to your care,' said God. 'Everything depends on you. You are my representative here on earth, among the animals. I have complete faith in you.' Then he added: 'I am just on my way to the kingdom of the insects, where Stag-Beetle is King. Like you, he is a perfect King: brave, wise, generous, tireless and kind.'

God raised his hand in salute, and was just about to disappear into the roots of a clump of grass when King Leo said: 'By the way, God, I had a strange dream.'

'What was it?' asked God. 'Perhaps I can tell you what it means.'

'I dreamed I was an outlaw, very dirty and ragged. I was murdering the animals and eating them. With a truly horrible hunger. I was called Leftovers. What does it mean?'

God laughed. 'That is easy. Dreams are memories of a former life. That was the life in which you got everything wrong. Now, as you see, you are getting everything right. Isn't it so?'

'It is,' said King Leo, puzzled. 'Yes, it is. I do seem to be getting everything right.'

God raised his hand again, smiled, and vanished into the grassroots.

Hyena handed King Leo his crown.

'It is time now,' said Hyena, 'for your Majesty to choose. Will you be carried through your kingdom on Elephant's back, or will you sleep?'

'Of course,' said King Leo. He felt sleepy, after the sausages. So there and then he closed his eyes and slept.

At that moment, all the animals breathed a sigh of relief. They got up off their knees and started doing what they usually did, playing and feeding.

All except the Wild Bull.

Now the Wild Bull stepped from the thorns. He stepped from the thorns, and the sun glistened on his blue-black body. There, at the edge of the thorns, he levelled his nose like a black stumpy cannon, and sniffed with his great black nostrils. His tail rose in the air and twirled its tassel. He was remembering his wife. He groaned softly and his dewlap trembled.

It seemed to him the murderer had been rewarded too well. He dragged his right hoof backward through the stony earth, and flung gravel up over his flank and back. Was King Leo going to be King for ever? Feasting on sausages, bowed to by all the animals, wearing a crown that looked like the starry heavens? He groaned louder, with a weird, hollow, booming sound, and flung more earth over his back. He glared at his enemy and the empty plate. This was not justice. To make a murderer King, this was not justice.

The Wild Bull stepped forward, slowly, till he stood right over the shaggy, sleeping King. His moment had come. With a flick of his horns, he tossed the crown into a swamp, where a watersnake grabbed it and sank out of sight with it, leaving a bubble.

Then he put his horns under the King and with one jerk tossed him into the top of a thorn tree – a big, strong-trunked thorn tree of ten million thorns.

'Leftovers!' he thundered. 'Leftovers! You have not paid for my wife. But now you shall pay.'

Leftovers woke up falling through the thorns, which

raked his body and clawed his face. But he did not hit the ground. He fell smack on to the Wild Bull's horns, who hurled him up again – back into the top of the thorn tree.

'Leftovers!' bellowed the Wild Bull. 'I am God's Judge. And Judgement Day has come!'

And again the torn and bleeding King fell through the dreadful tree, and again he fell on to the waiting horns, and it was as if he had fallen on to a trampoline. Up he went again, higher than ever, turning in the air, his legs outflung, as if he were no bigger than a rabbit, and the Wild Bull gazed up, his eyes flaming with joyful fury.

But as he came down through the whipping and slashing thorns for the third time, Leftovers grabbed the trunk and hung there. Was he awake or asleep? He shook his dazzled head. Where was his crown? Where was his kingdom? And his subjects? And his sausages? Where was God?

And there, clinging for dear life halfway up a thorn tree, above a demented Wild Bull, he knew he was Leftovers. And the rest was a dream. The crown, the sausages, the Hyena, the fanfare of Elephants, God – all were a dream.

But this was real. This real Wild Bull was the real husband of the real Wild Cow he really had killed and eaten. And these were real thorns.

He roared an enraged clap of thunder. And down below him the Wild Bull tore up the earth with his hooves, and he too bellowed thunder. God crouched in the grass clump, peering out between the fibres of the roots. 'All my fault!' he was muttering. 'All my fault!' as he tried to think what to do. But then the Wild Bull charged the tree. There came a crack, the earth jumped, and the whole tree blurred. In a shower of thorns, Leftovers dropped on to the Wild Bull's back, biting and clawing. The Wild Bull rolled over, but Leftovers sprang away, and with one bound he was gone – into the high grass where the Elephants too were hiding from the uproar, with their trunks curled into their mouths. The Wild Bull stormed and trampled in circles, hunting for Leftovers, tearing up small trees and bushes, till finally he stood panting, letting his red eyes slowly darken to a bright, burning black.

That was the end of King Leo's reign.

And now Leftovers roams the land as before, hungry as before, terrible as before. But he keeps out of the way of the Wild Bull, because the Wild Bull is ready for him, always sniffing for him, always alert.

And just as before, all the animals go in fear of Leftovers' unrolling carpet of thunder and his thunderbolt leap.

What can God do? He knows his trick would not work a second time. But it nearly had worked. If the Wild Bull had not burst out of the thorns, it might have worked. And so when Leftovers walks along the skyline at evening, when the sky flames red, God listens sadly. And all the animals listen too, as Leftovers' thunder rolls away across the plains and crumbles against the surrounding wall of sky.

'King Leo!' shouts Hyena, and laughs.

And Man, too, listens in his house. It seems to him that Leftovers' thunder is a sad sound. Peal after peal of thunder, shorter and shorter, ending in a few grunty coughs. Man can tell that Leftovers is remembering his dream of being King, his dream of being wise, generous, kind and beloved by all. 'Was it a dream?' says the first roll of thunder. 'Or was it real?' says the second. 'Or is this a dream now?' says the third. 'Or is this real?' says the fourth. And then, very fierce, as if he could hardly bear it, 'Was that a dream and is this real?' And after a pause: 'Or was that real and is this a dream?' Then shorter and shorter: 'Which is it? Which is it?' And shorter and shorter and shorter: 'Which? Which? Which?'

Then, in the silence, Leftovers frowns over the lump of sun behind his eyebrows. And he lowers his head, and half opens his mouth to cool the hunger of God that urges him forward.

The Dancers

A great, flaming star was falling. Owls looked up and the ball of fire, with its long tail, was reflected in their bulging eyes.

Most falling stars burn out to nothing, before they get near the earth. But this one did not. And the wide eyes of the Owls widened wider as the flaming ball grew and grew and – plunged silently into the dark mountains.

God was asleep. When dawn rose, he woke and started work, knowing nothing about the great star that had crashed into the Mountains.

Later that day God sighed and leaned back in his chair. His work just wasn't going right. He'd been trying for three days, and somehow it still wasn't right.

He'd been trying to make a Dancer. He wanted an animal that would dance for him. And what had he ended up with? A Cat!

There it sat, on his workbench, gazing at him sleepily out of slit eyes.

God lifted Cat down to the floor.

'Go on,' he said. 'Dance.'

Cat looked at him, lifted her tail straight, and gently curled and uncurled the tip of it.

'Is that all you can do?' asked God. 'You're my dancer. Dance.'

111

Cat yawned.

'I'm sleepy just now,' she said. 'It's quite hard work, you know, being created.'

And she settled down there and then, and closed her eyes.

God scratched his beard. He liked the look of Cat. And maybe she could dance as well as he'd hoped. But if she wouldn't, if she was just too lazy, what could he do about it?

He looked out through his window and rested his eyes on the mountains.

And now, as he gazed at those mountains, he noticed something different about them. They looked sick.

He went out on to the balcony to get a better view. Yes, they looked sick.

Then, in front of his eyes, they moved. It was like a hiccup. And again, they seemed to shrug.

What was going on? The Crow flew down on to his balcony rail.

Now the mountains were definitely up to something. They seemed to swell, then abruptly collapsed. They jigged. They shivered. They stretched up.

'The mountains are having some sort of fit,' said God. 'I wonder what's got into them?'

The Crow stared.

'I think,' said the Crow, 'I think they're trying to dance.'

God couldn't believe that. They both went on watching. And the mountains went on stretching and swaying and jigging. God could feel the vibration under his feet. Other creatures came out of the forest.

'It's an earthquake,' said Giraffe, bracing her legs wide.

And the birds flew up from the shuddering trees, till the whole sky was full of their circling, fluttering or gliding specks, all crying:

'What's got into the mountains?'

God set out to get a closer look. He arrived under the shadow of the mountains, and all the creatures were with him, and above him the birds. Even new-made Cat was there, peering from behind God's ankle.

Surely the Crow was right. Surely the mountains were dancing. At least they looked to be dancing.

Or they looked rather as if something inside them were dancing. As if creatures the size of the mountains were dancing under the gigantic fallen tent of the mountains, like people dancing under a great sheet.

But as they all watched, the mountains began to split. With a booming roar, a jagged crack ran up the rock face. The mountains were tearing themselves apart.

God watched that huge crack as it widened. Was something coming out? Were the mountains coming out from under the mountains?

It was an amazing sight, the eyes of God, and of all the creatures, all the birds, all the reptiles, so shining and round and still.

And there, out of the vast, gaping crevasse, came a tiny animal.

A dancing creature.

A Mouse!

It was a Mouse! A dancing Mouse!

The mountains became still. But the Mouse danced. He twirled, and leaped, and cavorted. He frisked, and jumped and twirled. God watched him, speechless with delight.

Mouse danced up to God and danced on to his hand. God held him up, on his palm. Cat saw the wide smile on God's face, and dug her claws into a root. She tore fibres from the root. Her teeth chattered together. She was sick with jealousy! God had made her as his very special dancer, and suddenly here was this Mouse!

'Mouse!' she hissed. 'A Mouse! A paltry, piddling, pitter-patter, pin-claw string-tail!'

And she buried her fangs in the root. Otherwise, she just might have leapt and swept the Mouse off God's hand with a single swipe of her thorny fist.

Back in God's workshop, Mouse became his favourite new creature. As God worked, Mouse danced at the end of the bench. He would leap and twirl, skip and frolic, with his long-fingered pink hands, and his elegant pink tail, and his black eyes so full of feeling.

Cat refused to come back to the workshop. She slunk through the forest. Passing a tree, she would suddenly lash out and rip a lump of bark clean off. 'The Mouse will pay. My day will come and Mouse will have to pay!' she yowled, and knocked the head off an orchid.

One day God was making Thrush. The voice-box of Thrush was in place. Perfect. Now the tongue. But as he eased the tongue into position – Barrummmmph!

The earth shook, just slightly.

Crow hammered on God's window.

'The mountains are at it again!' he cawed.

God frowned. He waited, without taking his eyes off the Thrush's tongue. He knew how vital it was to keep his eyes fixed on the job. And he didn't want to bungle this.

115

Nothing more happened. He gave the tongue its final touch. There!

And straight away – Barrrummmph! And the work-bench jolted so hard, Mouse, who had been cleaning his belly-fur, fell over and clutched the grain of the wood.

Crow hammered on the window. 'Come and see! It looks like another Mouse!'

God looked up then and saw the peaks shudder. He passed his hand over his brow and sighed. He really wanted to finish Thrush. He still had the most finicky job of all – fitting the song into the voice-box.

Then he saw Mouse gazing at him with excited eyes.

'Might it be another Mouse?' cried Mouse.

God smiled and nodded. 'Maybe a partner for you,' he said.

Mouse's nose began to tremble.

'A friend?' he squeaked.

'Who knows?' said God. 'Maybe a wife.'

'A wife!' cried Mouse. 'Oh, let me see her. Oh, are you sure?'

And Mouse leapt down on to the floor, and scampered towards the doorway. He stopped, waiting for God.

'You go on,' said God. 'I'll sit here and finish what I'm doing. Bring your wife back here.'

Mouse was already running.

'But mind,' shouted God after him, laughing, 'don't bring anybody else. If it isn't another Mouse, tell it to go back where it came from. We don't want it.'

Mouse raced through the forest, with wildly beating heart. No, he wouldn't bring anybody else back. He was already imagining the fantastic dances he would soon be having with his partner – with his wife!

From every corner of the forest, the creatures came

hurrying towards the mountains. Last time it had been so comical! After all that tremendous commotion of mountains, to see nothing come out but a tiny midget Mouse – even if it was a dancing Mouse.

This time, all the creatures agreed, the mountains were dancing even more wildly. If it was dancing. They seemed to swell, and flop down. Then great bulges raced from one end to the other. Sometimes it looked as if the whole range was going to lift off and jig in the air.

Mouse too, standing there, out in front of all the other creatures, jigged and hopped with impatience.

'It's my wife!' he called. 'She's on her way! She's dancing through the darkness towards us. Yes, yes! I remember what it's like in there. Pretty frightening, I can tell you. You have to dance, or you just might get too frightened.'

And cupping his tiny, pink hands to his mouth he squealed: 'Hurry up, my darling wife!'

But no crack appeared in the rock face. The mountains went on shivering, squirming and teetering. They tossed their tops, like horns. They surged, like trees in a storm. They almost swirled like water. But still no crack.

Mouse had become still and silent. Was something wrong? Why was it taking so long?

Suddenly a Mongoose barked and pointed. A tiny crack had appeared in a great slab of cliff. Had it been there before?

'It's beginning! The hills are going to hatch!' screamed the Cockatoo.

At last Mouse couldn't stand it any longer. He snatched up a stalk of dry grass, ran forward, pushed one end of the stalk into the fine crack, and heaved on

117

the other with all his strength, as if it were a crowbar.

The boom was so stunning, so immense, that all the animals cowered. It really sounded as if the mountains had exploded. And sure enough, the cliffs were tearing apart.

And out of the gaping rent in the cliffs came –

Elephants!

Dancing Elephants!

Great flapping and cracking ears, great coiling and swinging trunks, great swooshing and sweeping tusks, great looming and frowning foreheads, great baggy and bouncing bodies, great stamping and trampling feet!

They danced out over the creatures. How many? It seemed to the poor creatures, flattened in the dust, rolling in the dust, whirling in the dust, that the mountains were turning into Elephants, as if there'd be nothing left after this but the skin of the empty mountains lying flat on the earth. Howls and shrieks went up, and trees fell splintering down, showering monkeys, marmosets, martens and squirrels, not to speak of Owls' eggs. Wildly, not caring at all where their huge flatteners came down, the Elephants danced.

'Help!' came the cry of the creatures of the world. 'Oh God, help us!'

But far away in his workshop God was bowed over the open throat of the Thrush. He wasn't even aware of the tremor of the chair he sat in.

While the creatures whirled about, this way and that, under the whirling dance of the Elephants.

But Mouse was coming to his senses.

Where was his wife? After all his hopes, where was his wife?

He leaped up among the Elephants. And in his tiny voice, with terrific fury, he squeaked:

'Where is my wife?'

The effect was unbelievable. The whole churning mass of Elephants came to a dead stop.

'Who are you all?' squeaked Mouse. 'We don't want you. God doesn't want you, he wants my wife. God has ordered you to get back under the mountains, get back where you came from. Get straight back there and SEND ME MY WIFE.'

The effect of this astonished even the furious Mouse. With trumpetings of fear, with ears flung back over their shoulders, with trunks curled up tight above their heads or stretched out forwards, the Elephants scattered. Anywhere but back under the mountains! At top speed, in every direction, they bolted.

They didn't want to go back under the black mountains. Anywhere but that. So they simply fled, out across the bright world. They smashed broad roads through the forest, and where the jungle was too dense they surfed over the top, like great power-boats, and now, hearing their screams of panic, God looked up from the throat of the Thrush.

He frowned. What a hideous uproar in the world! And surely that was the voice of the Mouse! Yes, it was the shouting of Mouse, as he hurtled through the trees, chasing the Elephants with 'Where's my wife?' and 'God doesn't want you. Get back where you came from and send my wife,' and then again, louder than ever, the fleeing screams of the poor Elephants.

The Elephants faded away into the edges of the world. The rest of the creatures couldn't stop talking about it.

What a fantastic thing, the fury of the Mouse. With a single shout, he had scattered a whole mountain range of Elephants!

But Mouse himself was heartbroken. He dragged his tail along. He didn't want to dance for God any more. He went back to look at the ruined and shattered mountains. Was his wife somewhere under all that? It didn't look as if the mountains would ever dance again. It didn't look as if they had anything left.

He crept into Man's house. He made his home in a crack in the wall, under Man's bed. And at night he crept out quietly, to eat Man's crumbs. He danced no more.

God missed his Mouse. Cat had begun to dance for him now. Just now and again, especially in the evening. But it wasn't the same. Once you've seen a dancing Mouse a Cat seems just clumsy.

One day, as he was kneading a bit of clay, God was thinking about his Mouse. He wondered what had happened to him. Nobody seemed to know. All the animals agreed he must have been flattened into the clay by the foot of an Elephant. But suddenly, as he sat there thinking, God realized what his fingers had done. They had made a Mouse.

Carefully, he breathed life into the tiny, perfect creature.

She stood up on his hand. She lifted her little arms. And to God's absolute delight, she began to dance.

Cat could not believe it. She clamped her jaws tight shut, so that the boiling steam of her rage shouldn't flash hissing across the room. Then she made one leap. Cat cleared God's hand, like a horse going over a fence, but Mouse was already out through the doorway.

Cat leaped again, but Mouse was already in the forest. Cat leaped through the leaves, but Mouse was already among Man's carrots. And as Cat leaped again, Mouse shot in through Man's doorway.

Cat came in so fast her claws tore splinters from the floorboards, but Mouse was already down the hole, under Man's bed.

And at that moment, Man's wife appeared with a broom, and saw the strange animal with its hair all on end, its eyes like raging lamps, its white fangs bared, and she thought: 'That looks nasty.' And with one whack of her broom she swept Cat back out among the carrots.

Down the hole, the Mouse from God's hands dashed straight into the arms of the Mouse from the Mountains.

Think of their happiness!

Each evening, after supper, while they lay in their bed together, Man would play his flute to Woman. He played softly. And under the bed, the two Mice held each other tightly and listened. After the flute had fallen silent, the two Mice came out from under the bed, out on to the middle of the floor, and there in the firelight they began to dance.

The first evening, Woman, lying half asleep, saw them, and shook Man gently. 'Look!' she whispered. 'What are those?'

Then Man and Woman lay there, watching the two Mice dancing in the firelight.

And so it happened each evening. Man would play his flute softly to Woman, and afterwards they would lie quietly and watch, till the two tiny creatures came out from under the bed and began to dance together, in the middle of the room, in the firelight. And their happiness was so great, as they danced, that even God became aware of it. He lay awake, unable to sleep, tossing and turning, and muttering: 'Something is keeping me awake! What can it be? Something strange is going on somewhere. I can feel it. But where is it? And what is it?' And he had the feeling that somewhere in his Creation, somehow, there was a huge happiness hidden from him.

And strangely enough, the Elephants could feel it too. They didn't know what it was, but out in the forest, as the stars rose, they became more and more restless, and shifting from great foot to great foot they began to dance. And under the flickering stars the jumbled range of mountains began to dance softly. The whole night was filling up with the happiness of the Mice, as they danced in the firelight. While Man and Woman, gazing out from under their bedclothes with the flames of the fire reflecting in their eyes, watched them. Till God had to get out of bed, muttering: 'What is keeping me awake? What is it?' And he paced to and fro in his bedroom, and stood at his window and stared out over the forests at the hills, and at the shaking stars above the hills, and again he walked to and fro, his arms clasped tightly across his chest and his eyes glittering.